BLACK SEAS OF INFINITY

THE R'LYEH CYCLE
BOOK TWO

Edited by William Holloway

JOURNALSTONE
YOUR LINK TO ARTIST TALENT

ISBN: 978-1-68510-127-5 (sc)
ISBN: 978-1-68510-128-2 (ebook)

First printing edition: June 28, 2024
Printed by JournalStone Publishing in the United States of America.
Cover Artwork and Design: Mikio Murakami
Edited by Sean Leonard
Proofreading, Interior Layout, and Cover Layout by Scarlett R. Algee

JournalStone Publishing
3205 Sassafras Trail
Carbondale, Illinois 62901

JournalStone books may be ordered through booksellers or by contacting:
www.journalstone.com

BLACK SEAS OF INFINITY

THE R'LYEH CYCLE
BOOK TWO

AND THE WHOLE OF REALITY SHALL CRASH UPON ME

Curtis M. Lawson

For David, Pete, and Trey, whose music helped
me discover the path to R'lyeh.

Thank you to William, Gemma, and Brett for sharing
these pages with me and to Scarlett and the
JournalStone crew for their hard work.

.

I GLIDE THROUGH the cold black water. Hunger such as I have never known spurs me forward. Emotions so powerful that they have no name compel me to stalk the flooded ground-level of my apartment building.

My movements are fluid, possessed of an inhuman grace. I feel lithe and strong—superhuman even. A hundred sensations overwhelm me. I can taste and smell through my limbs. Neurons fire throughout my entire body. My vision is sharp and acute, even in the murky water.

The power is out, and little light filters in from the outside. Water comes up to above the doorknobs of all the apartments in the hall. The units are abandoned, of course, so this place is mine now. The darkness and solitude soothe me, even as my mind threatens to unravel beneath the pressure of the intense emotions that thunder in my hearts and rattle in my mind—distant cousins of love and hate, but infinitely deeper and more complex.

I'm dragging a struggling child behind me. I don't know the boy's name, but I've seen him from my window before, always in the company of his mother. There's something wrong with him—something off in his gait and posture.

I caress the boy's face, taking stock of his features. He's odd in that regard as well. His face is too flat, and his eyes are an unusual shape.

My arm is constricted around the boy's head, muting his screams, but he thrashes in the water. Small hands pull at my grip, but the resistance is a moot gesture.

A terrible mixture of sensations assaults me as I drag the child along. The boy's skin tastes like cigarette smoke and neglect. Backed-up sewage pipes spill piss and shit into the flooded hall. And then there is the nauseating smell of ammonia that bleeds from my own flesh.

The chain lock to apartment 107 keeps it from opening more than a few inches. I flatten my body and squeeze through the small space, strong yet formless. I'm reminded of the words of Bruce Lee: Be water, my friend.

I suddenly find myself stuck. It takes me a moment to figure out why, but then it hits me. The child will not fit through the small gap. I silently curse, then reach out of the water and unfasten the chain lock. Once I've pulled the boy into the flooded apartment, I lock the door behind us.

The apartment holds different smells than the hallway did. A potpourri of spoiled fruit and black mold dances in the air with the visceral odors of blood and rotten meat.

I release the boy and vanish beneath the water. The child gasps for air and struggles to stand. The water only comes to the boy's chest, but he still thrashes about as if he might drown. I savor every moment of his sobbing and shaking. His fear is intoxicating.

He calls out for his mother, his words slow and drawn out. I breach the surface and repeat him in a mocking tone. The boy falls backward in panic and sucks in a mouthful of the putrid water.

I dart across the room as he pukes up the water he'd sucked in. I scuttle over a mound of offal and climb up the wall. There I wait for the boy to finish heaving.

The child wipes his mouth and calls for his mother once more. I echo his words again, in a shrill, mocking tone. He glances this way, trying to see through the oppressive darkness.

My skin takes on a glow, the cells bursting with emerald radiance. My bioluminescence illuminates a mound of carnage below me—dismembered bits of cats, and rats, and men. Dead eyes from a dozen corpses reflect my jade light into the room.

The boy stares at me above my totem of flesh, his mouth agape. He is too scared to even scream. I mock him again.

"Mama! Mama! Mama!"

Thunder echoes from outside and rain pelts the windows of the apartment, almost in rhythm with my evil mockery.

Satisfied with the boy's terror, I dive back into the water. One by one by one, my arms coil around his legs and drag him under. My limbs—of which there are all too many—constrict around the child, crushing his bones. He tries to scream, but water fills his lungs and silences his voice.

A cloud of blood washes over me as I pluck the boy's limbs off with disturbing ease. I taste his life essence wash across my entire body. The sensation is too much for me—more intense than the best high or the finest meal or the wildest sex. I succumb to total sensory overload and white light overtakes the room, as if I'm living through some 16 mm film burn.

***

I'm stolen from my dream by the lightning strobing through the sides of my curtains and thunder playing an arrhythmic beat outside.

Rain taps furiously against the windows. The storm's been going for well over a week, and the incessant pitter-patter is a constant reminder of the overwhelming vastness of the world beyond my apartment. I imagine the glass eroding, raindrop by raindrop, until it gives way, and the enormity of existence floods in and crashes upon me.

Normally I would put on some music to take my mind off such a dreadful nightmare and drown out the sound of the storm, but the power's been out for most of the week. No electricity means no TV, no phone, no computer. All I have is a battery-powered AM/FM radio, and I don't know how long those AAs are going to last.

It's dark out, and I'm not sure if it's morning or night, not that it matters. The sky has been overcast ever since whatever happened happened. Some of the radio stations say it was a meteor crashing on the other side of the world. Others claim it was a nuke. One guy on NPR suggested it was a massive carbon eruption released from a melting glacier. Whatever's going on out there, the sun hasn't shined in a week. The nights are moonless black affairs, and the days are only marginally brighter.

Even before the entire East Coast flooded and the power went out, time held little meaning to me. It's been years since I've been outside of my apartment. I'm lucky enough to make my living as a comic artist, which means I can work from home. My food mainly consists of MREs, frozen dinners, and canned vegetables that I have delivered once every two months. It's been almost five years since I've gone on a date. Three since I've seen a friend in person. Six months since my mother last visited. Needless to say, times and dates mean little to me, aside from meeting deadlines.

I groan as I walk to the window, the wide beam of my flashlight guiding the way. My limbs feel so stiff, my motion stinted. With every clumsy step, I yearn for the fluid, graceful movement of my dream-self. I can still almost feel that supple strength, like phantom limb syndrome, but for a whole other body.

Casting aside the blinds, I take stock of the outside world. All I see is black at first—terrible darkness of such enormity that it makes my knees buckle. A flash of lightning pushes the darkness back and reveals the briefest glimpse of a flooded cityscape. Street signs stick out of the water like buoys, and the roofs of trucks breach the surface like sandbars.

Almost as quickly as it struck, the lightning retreats. I stare into the darkness once more, but only for a few moments before another lightning strike illuminates the sky. The white flash washes all color from the scene, leaving the bricks of the neighboring buildings as colorless as the mortar that joins them. Discarded bottles and cans float on the water alongside serpentine strands of yellow police tape, the bright colors of the detritus muted by the lightning's fierce illumination.

White ripples disrupt the black surface as if something waits just beneath. The imagery evokes thoughts of diseased rats with mangy fur and slithering eels with slick, shiny flesh. It makes me think of childhood monsters—make-believe things that yearn to be real and clamber under beds or in the shadows of closets.

I stand in front of my window for several minutes, gazing upon the tug of war between light and dark. One moment the city is a sea of black, starless and unplugged; a few seconds later, I'm greeted with snapshots of canals that were once streets before the boundless sea and endless storm rolled in to claim them. I'm not sure which frightens me more: the endless darkness, or the landscape it hides. Both could sweep me into oblivion and scatter my very being as if it was so much sand.

With my daily dose of exposure therapy checked off, I shut the curtains and turn toward the kitchen. I turn on the radio, and the sound of rain falls behind the hiss of FM static. It takes some fiddling with the dial until I find something worth stopping on—an old Roy Orbison tune that just barely cuts through the static. I light a candle on the table and open an MRE without looking at the label. Inside is a sausage patty and hashbrowns. Since it's breakfast laid out before me, and since I just woke up, I decide to call it morning.

There's a knock on my door, and I nearly choke. My heart races and my head pounds. I consider shutting off the radio before they hear it. But what if they already did hear it, and the sound suddenly dies off? Then they'll know I'm here, and they'll know I'm awake.

"Sam?" a voice calls out, followed by another knock. It's Daryll Jackson, the building superintendent. He's a nice enough guy by all accounts, but not nice enough for me to open the door to him.

I hold my breath and pray for him to leave. No such luck, of course. He knocks again, then starts talking through the door.

"I know you don't like being bothered, Sam, but a bunch of us are pooling our resources to try and get through the flood. God knows when we'll be able to get to a store, and some folks are running low on basics like food and toilet paper. I was hoping you might want to throw in with us."

I suck in ragged breaths, trying to stay as quiet as possible. In my mind's eye, I see Daryll with a crowbar and a mob of my neighbors behind him. They're ready to bust in here and take my food for themselves. I know that's not the case. I know I'm being unreasonable. But what if...?

"I'm not sure if you can hear me, Sam, but I know you stock up on food, and there are some young kids in the building who are about to go hungry. Amy on the second floor is pregnant and eating for two."

I tiptoe to the door, lighting my way with the flashlight so I don't trip. I look out through the peephole. Daryll is standing there, his body-builder frame illuminated by the light of an electric lantern in his hand. He looks tired and haggard. The harsh light doesn't do him any favors.

"If you want to help out...or if you need something yourself, you know where to find me."

Daryll walks away, and the light from his lantern fades until my view through the peephole turns black. I gasp in relief and rest my head against the door. The stress of the whole encounter has me dizzy and lightheaded.

It's not that I don't want to help, or that I'm hoarding supplies. I can't open the door for him though. I can't have him in my house or hold a conversation. I can't look him in the eye and wonder what secret thoughts run through his mind.

I look back toward the kitchen. My food is highlighted by the wavering aura of the candle flame, but there's no way I'm eating now. My nerves are shot and my stomach is in knots.

***

I've spent the last several hours working. NYC is experiencing the same floods and power outages that we're seeing in Providence, so my publisher has pushed back all deadlines. Still, there's no reason to procrastinate. I'm an old-school doodler. Wacom tablets just don't feel right to me, so I still work with blue pencils, Micron pens, and Bristol paper; thus I don't need the power on to do my job. Plus, it will be nice to be ahead of the game when this all blows over. Maybe I can even find the time for a few commissions.

The process is painfully slow given the conditions. The eye strain from working by candlelight is giving me a migraine, and I can't concentrate worth a damn. My mind is cluttered with a dozen species of anxiety, and it's coming through in my drawing. The lines on my paper are sloppy and erratic, and the perspective is warped.

I lay the pencil down and stand to stretch my back before walking around my apartment for a few moments. Looking outside, I can see that the sky has lightened to a sort of dusky charcoal—a sign that the sun still exists above the dense storm clouds. It's just bright enough to see the flooded streets without the aid of lightning strikes, and I notice people taking advantage of this sad facsimile of daylight.

A group of men wade through chest-high water to loot a 7-Eleven on the corner. They scramble for batteries and plastic-packaged junk food that hasn't been ravaged by the water. White ripples and wakes color the water around them, and I once again wonder what things may swim in these flooded streets. I imagine being out there with these men, trudging through that cold water and feeling a wharf rat nudge against my arm. The thought sends a chill through my body.

I couldn't go out there, even if I was starving, but these guys are made of sterner stuff. I'm guessing they have families—people who depend on them. I wonder if their children will be living off rationed Slim-Jims and Doritos. A twinge of guilt washes over me as I watch them and remember Daryll asking me to share my food with some of the other tenants.

Maybe that's why I had that terrible dream about killing that boy—a sort of guilt manifestation for hiding in here with my hoard of MREs and canned veggies while children and pregnant women go hungry.

Daryll is right. I can help out, and I should. I don't need to interact with anyone to do so. I'll just leave some food out in the hall with a note on it, and he can grab it the next time he goes knocking on doors to check up on people.

I pack up a shopping bag with MREs, a jar of peanut butter, and some canned corn and green beans. I scrawl out a note that reads, *I hope this helps,* and staple it to the bag. Now all I have to do is open the door.

"Just open the door..."

What if Daryll is out there waiting? What if he tries to talk to me? My throat grows dry just imagining it. Even worse, what if he sees this food and decides he wants it all? Is there any way I could stop him? I don't think there is.

"Just open the door..."

Something creaks as I move forward. Rationally, I know it's the floorboards contracting because of the cold. A little part of me thinks it may have come from my apartment door though—the brass hinges and the wooden frame protesting against the weight of the outside world pressing against them.

"Just open the door..."

The wind howls outside my window. But what if that wailing is actually coming from the hall? What if something waits across the threshold, some beast born of my broken mind and brought into the real world through shadow and storm?

"I can do this..."

I press my head against the door, taking deep and conscious breaths. I can feel the pressure of all of reality pushing against the door. The wood pulses beneath my touch, ready to buckle at any moment. Bile rises in my throat even as I tell myself that it's all in my head.

The universe isn't going to crash over me like a tsunami if I open the door. There's nothing and no one out there.

No one waiting in the hall to judge me.

No one skulking in the dark, waiting for the chance to make me feel stupid and small.

No one lurking in the shadows, ready to ambush me as soon as I open the door.

I inhale and concentrate on steadying my body. I exhale and will my heart to slow.

Inhale—I focus on the tension in my neck and shoulders. Exhale—I will them to relax.

Inhale—My attention shifts to the seismic quivering in my limbs. Exhale—the trembling mellows to the point where I could almost blame it on the unseasonable chill.

"I can do this..."

I throw the deadbolt and grip the knob. The brass is cold to the touch, much colder than it should be. Images of that offal totem pole from my dream—that ghastly sculpture formed of flesh and fur, bone and entrails—flash across my imagination. I feel it out there, somewhere beyond the door to my apartment. It's watching and waiting.

"I can't do this..."

I lock the deadbolt and press my head against the door again.

***

The rubber residue from a hundred erased lines is piled up at the corner of my drawing desk. I look down at the musclebound anti-hero on the page. He's strong and confident. He's handsome, daring, and capable. Sure, he's nothing but a collection of blue lines on Bristol—an adolescent power fantasy trapped in a two-dimensional world—but I can't help but feel that he has more value than I do as a living, breathing person.

I live and speak and think, yet this make-believe character will have such a deeper impact on the world than I can ever hope. He was old when I was a child, and he'll be captivating minds long after I'm dead. My great gift to the world—my contribution to human history—is to serve as a conduit for make-believe things to manifest themselves in the real world. I'm not sure if that's beautiful or pathetic. I suspect it's both.

The script calls for a splash page where our hero stands atop a mountain of corpses. He smirks at me from the paper, so cocksure and perfect. I can't stand to look at him, so I turn my attention to rendering the mound of dead flesh. The scene takes place on a battlefield, so the fallen should bear wartime wounds, but I find myself making things more gruesome than the writer intended.

The corpses I draw are incomplete things—scraps of bodies, arranged with diabolical intention. The spinal cord jutting from the base of one jawless skull is braided with that of another. The cheeks of corpses are slit and pinned back, exposing rows of broken teeth. A wall of headless, limbless torsos forms the base, and mangled fetuses are shoved between them like mortar between bricks.

It's not just human wreckage that I draw into the mountain of corpses. There are parts of horses and oxen, dogs and rats. A hundred eyes stare out from the mass of flesh, hatred eerily rendered into each.

It's been hard for me to draw since the flooding began and the power went out. This time it's different. I render this abomination with no problem at all. My pencil moves without thought or doubt. I don't reach for my eraser even once.

I lean back and look at the page. Only now do I realize that it's so much like the thing from my dream—that sculpture of skin and meat and bone—that tribute to madness and sadism. It's hideous and beautiful, repugnant and captivating. I'm hyper-critical of my work, generally speaking, but I can't take my eyes away from the page. I stare transfixed and disgusted upon this image and wonder how such a thing ever appeared in my mind.

Only a sudden noise—footsteps and mutterings from the hallway—stirs me from my reverie. I push the page aside and turn my gaze toward the door. What's out there now?

My heart is in my throat, because I'm a rabbit-nerved mess, but I skulk toward the door. I've been sitting down at my desk for hours, so my knees crack and I'm reminded of the stiff, inelegant nature of my anatomy. I curse the failings of my body as I think of the barbarian from my comic page, so powerful and sure. I think of the strength and grace I possessed in my dream last night. What I would give for a healthy body and a sure mind.

I press my eye to the peephole and peer through. A feminine silhouette is barely visible—her black clothes and blacker hair are almost one with the darkness. Only the pale flesh of her arms, those spots of negative space between twisting spirals of black ink, reflect any of the dim, ashen light coming from the hallway windows. She's mumbling something as she fumbles with her keys in one hand and a garbage bag in the other.

I imagine her turning and smiling seductively—black lips upturned, exposing white, predatory teeth. In my mind she whispers a challenge, daring me to cross my threshold and follow across hers.

She doesn't do that, of course. She never does.

Would it matter if she did? Maybe if I was a normal fucking person, but I'm not. I'm an anxiety-ridden chickenshit who wouldn't be able to chase his dreams if they beckoned him with a black-lacquered fingernail.

I watch from my peephole as she goes into her apartment and shuts the door, just as I have a hundred times before. I know that sounds creepy, and I suppose it is, but I'm not some perverted stalker. I just like to imagine being with her. I can't have a real relationship or go out on dates, so I create scenarios in my head, and if I'm going to have a make-believe girlfriend, it might as well be the gorgeous, unattainable goth girl from across the hall.

Her name is Aisling, not that we've ever met or been introduced. I don't know her, but I feel like I do. I've picked up little things about her from watching and listening. She only gets her caffeine from independent coffee shops, never Starbucks or Dunkin Donuts. She reads comics, mostly horror stuff like *Locke & Key* and *Eerie*—not the biceps and boobs stuff that I draw. Her music taste ranges from old Rat Pack stuff to synthwave, though I hear the occasional pop song leak out from her apartment.

I'd like to say I haven't stalked her online, but I have, and to little avail. I guess that makes me twice the loser for trying and failing. All her social media is private, but I did find that she's originally from Dayton, Ohio, and she dropped out of Roger Williams here in Rhode Island.

The rest of the stuff—her personality, affectations, quirks, fears, and yearnings—I kind of filled in the blanks for myself there. Yes, I'm aware that the version of Aisling I've created in my mind is as much a fantasy as our relationship, but I'm okay with that. Daydreaming about my made-up version of her does no harm, at least not to her. My therapist would say the fantasy is bad for my mental well-being. I'm guessing she would say that anyway, but I haven't been to therapy in a long time.

I think it's healthy to occasionally escape into the happy thoughts of unreality. What did Milton say? The mind is its own place and can make a heaven of hell... Something like that. What's a better way to occupy myself, playing out a scenario in the theater of my mind where I have the guts to leave my house and be in the presence of another human being—a sexy, intelligent, sensitive woman—or dwelling on the lonely reality of my pathetic existence?

Her scent permeates the water and awakens me—the alluring mix of pheromones, sweat, and oil beneath a mask of lavender and oakmoss. It's Aisling. I shouldn't know what she smells like, but I do.

I creep out from a mound of debris—a small shelter made up of broken furniture, beer cans, and soggy cardboard. I stretch my limbs around myself like a star, then pull them in tight as I slip through the narrow gap between the chain-locked door and the frame.

"Samael?" Her voice echoes from the stairwell. I wonder why she calls me by that name, but deep down I know why. Fear of my kind has been drilled into the ancestral memory of these apes. We are the muse for their infernal fiends and their terrible angels alike. It's no wonder she calls me a demon's name.

My kind? What the hell am I talking about?

"Samael? Are you down here?" she calls out into the dark hallway. Her voice trembles, but I think it's with excitement rather than fear. Some part of me, a level of consciousness behind my own, finds this amusingly foolish.

"I've brought you a gift...a sacrifice."

I swim toward her voice and her smell. She stands in waist-high water at the bottom of the stairs, her pale skin almost aglow in the dim light. The lower half of her dress flows and billows beneath the surface—an ebony octopus amid a black ocean. The top part of her dress, the half above the water, is soaked as well, and it clings to her chest and belly. Her hair hangs in wet strands about her bare shoulders, and her eyes hold a lunatic gleam behind her smeared makeup. I have never seen anyone look so sexy.

She clutches a plastic garbage bag. Something moves within it, desperate to escape. I can't smell it through the plastic, but I pray for it to be a person...a baby or an infant. It's an aberrant wish, I realize this, but even as I shudder at the thought, it fills me with hunger and excitement.

Of course, it's not a human in the bag. It's too small to be any larger than a baby, and it struggles with too much strength and vigor for that to be the case.

No, it's some other animal. Still, some sacrifice is better than none. I reach out of the murk and coil my arm around the bag. I graze her hand and goosebumps erupt up her arms. She gasps and bites her lip.

I vanish into the dark water, leaving her to crave my touch. The creature Aisling has delivered to me thrashes within the bag as I drag it below the surface. I pin it to the floor with two arms, crushing the air from its lungs. Its ribs break beneath, and I force it to gasp for breath—to suck in the filthy water of the flooded hallway. Its struggle gives way to a series of violent seizures and then to stillness. I cast the dead thing aside and turn my attention back to Aisling.

"Sam?" she calls again, but this time it's my name...my real name. I've imagined that single syllable coming off her lips so many times. To hear it for real sends a tremor of excitement through my soul.

I reach between her thighs with two limbs and nudge her legs apart. She eagerly obliges. I run an arm— No, a tentacle... I run a tentacle up her calf and thigh, my suckers peppering her soft flesh with tiny kisses. The other encircles her leg and climbs up to her ass. I pull her toward me and she moans the way I always imagined she would.

Lust and hatred wash over me. I want to fuck her and love her. I want to drown her and eat her. Part of me worships her, while another part finds her revolting, primitive, and alien.

She urges me on as I explore her body. All my limbs are upon her, climbing her body like ivy. She tears her dress down, exposing her breasts, and tugs at the silver rings in her nipples. My tentacle lays a dozen kisses on her clit as I invade her sex. She cries out for Jesus and I feel her tighten upon me.

Aisling begs me to fill her and possess her. She mutters prayers, not to the God of men, but to someone much older.

"Praise be you... You alone among the stars..."

I press another limb against her ass, teasing her with the promise of more of me. Her prayer is broken by a moan.

"...you alone in the deep..."

She emphasizes the last word and falls back against the stairs. She arches her back, leaving only her head and chest above the water. She bucks her hips into me, driving me deeper into her. Her eyes roll back until I only see the whites, framed by smears of black makeup. Ebony lips curl back to reveal white teeth clamped down on her pink tongue. She claws at the wall as her entire body tenses.

"...you alone in the dark!"

***

A knocking at the door awakens me. The carnal ecstasy of my dream evaporates as I find myself alone in the dark. The feelings of confidence and nimble strength are overridden by aches and pains laced with anxiety. Reality weighs down on me like a boulder, reminding me in a not-so-gentle fashion that such primal pleasure is solely the province of imagination, at least for me.

Another knock echoes from the front door. A shiver goes through me as I ponder who or what is outside my apartment.

"One minute!" I shout, hoping that will quell the rapping.

I stumble out of my bed and realize that my dream has left me with a raging erection that is quite noticeable through my pajama pants. I throw on an oversized sweatshirt that hangs past my crotch and make my way into the living room.

"Sam!" I freeze at the sound of Daryll's voice calling from outside my apartment. "Please open the door! It's important!"

There's an urgency to his tone. Something's wrong, or maybe it's a ruse. Either way, I can tell that he won't go away unless I answer.

He knocks again as a hundred tiny raindrops rap at my window. It feels like my little keep is under siege from the outside world—barbarians slamming on the gates and battering the walls. The thought robs me of my breath.

"I know it's late, but we've got a real problem, man."

"Coming..." I try to shout it, but my voice comes out as a whisper.

I suck in shallow breaths as I approach the front door. The apartment is pitch-black, save for the light of intermittent lightning strikes outside. I slowly navigate my living room by memory, trying not to trip or bump into anything.

Through the peephole, I see Daryll's face. He looks ghoulish in the bluish illumination of the LED lantern he carries. I swallow and once again tell him I'll be one moment.

Steeling myself, I reach out for the brass deadbolt and find it cold to the touch. My fingers tremble as I open the lock, and shivers radiate through my entire body at the sound of it clicking.

Halfway there. I can do this. I can open the door.

I reach for the doorknob, but my hand freezes in place an inch away. My heart is racing and a feeling of nausea creeps over me. Why is he here? What does he want?

"Sam?"

I slowly exhale and force myself to unlock the bottom lock. I leave the chain lock in place and open the door just as far as the chain will allow.

Daryll is even more intimidating than he looked through the weird, fisheye lens distortion of the peephole. He looks like someone I'd draw in one of my comics—all muscle and confidence. He almost reminds me of Luke Cage—not the 70s *Heroes for Hire* version with a tiara, but the Brian Michael Bendis revamp. It occurs to me that he could easily kick this door open if he wanted, chain lock be damned.

"Yes?" I ask, immediately wondering if I sounded rude. I didn't mean to come across that way, but I'm pretty sure I did. He probably thinks I'm an asshole. I bet they all do.

"Have you seen or heard anything weird? Maybe a kid playing in the halls? Or a struggle of any kind?"

"Umm...no. Not that I can think of. Is everything okay?"

"A kid from the second floor went missing—Danny Echols. Do you know him?"

"I don't think so," I say. "I don't really know anyone."

Daryll nods. I can't place the look in his eyes. Maybe it's pity. Maybe it's judgment. It could also be suspicion.

"His mom's a mess right now. Danny's got Down syndrome and a bucketful of health problems."

Down syndrome? I do know the kid he's talking about. I've seen him from my window, standing outside with his mother, waiting for the school bus to pick him up. I've seen him in my dreams, dragged beneath the water and torn to pieces. But that wasn't real...

"If he wandered off in the storm or the flood... Well, it's not good. Ms. Echols says he wouldn't just run off though."

There's a moment of silence, and I'm not sure what Daryll wants from me. We stare at each other, as if in some silent standoff.

"Well, I hope he turns up," I say, breaking the silence. "If I notice anything I'll let you know."

"This is kind of awkward, Sam, but I told Ms. Echols I'd check everyone's apartments. I don't think anyone here is a perv or anything, but you never know, right? I mean, BTK was the president of his church council."

He wants to come in. Fuck...fuck...fuck...

"Don't worry if things are a mess. It's not like any of us can take out the trash or anything right now."

Why would he say that? Does he think I'm a hoarder? Does he think I wallow in my own filth? I bet they all think that. I bet they all talk about it—how I probably live in a labyrinth of pizza boxes among rats and roaches.

"Soooo?"

I try to answer Daryll, but my voice falters. I close my eyes and lower my head while taking a deep breath before trying to speak again.

"Of course." The words croak past my tightening throat. "One moment."

I close the door and rest my fingertips against the chain lock. I have to open it, I know. What will it look like if I don't? But I don't want this man in my home. I don't want anyone in here.

"Rip off the band-aid," I whisper to myself.

I pull the chain taut, then let it fall. Bile rises from my stomach as I open the door and motion for Daryll to come in—to invade my sanctum.

He crosses my threshold, lantern in hand. I've never been this close to him before, and I don't think I realized exactly how big he is. He's got the better part of a foot on me, and outweighs me by at least fifty pounds. If he decided right here and now that he wanted my food, my water, or my life, there is nothing I could do to stop him. What a wretched thing it is to feel helpless.

Daryll walks around my living room, casting his lantern behind my sofa and under the table, as if I might have some poor, hogtied child just lying around. He makes small talk—mumblings about the rain and the flood—as he approaches my drawing desk. The white light washes over the pages I've been working on. He picks up the splash page and eyes the mound of corpses.

"Wow, that is some brutal shit! Very cool, man!" His eyes don't say *cool*, they say *Wow, maybe this guy is a pervert child snatcher.* "Kind of messed up, but still cool. You drew this?"

"Yes." I nod, then turn my gaze to the floor. "Please be careful with them. The ink can smudge and they take a long time to create."

Daryll returns the Bristol board to my desk. He asks if this is what I do for a living. He doesn't care, of course. It's just B.S. to keep things from getting too awkward. I play his game and list the titles I've been on. I somehow doubt he's heard of any of them. He doesn't strike me as a fanboy.

He makes his way into my kitchen and I see him eyeing my food, taking stock of my supplies. I find myself wondering if there really is a missing kid, or if he's just scoping out my apartment so he can steal from me later.

"I meant to leave some MREs outside for you, those ones in the bag on the counter." I can barely find the breath to speak. "Feel free to take them on your way out."

"That's mighty generous of you, Sam." His smile isn't quite insincere, but it's restrained—a bit cynical even.

Daryll moves on to check my bathroom, casting aside the shower curtain and looking in the linen closet. The tour finally concludes in my room, where he finds neither a kidnapped child nor a molested corpse.

"Thanks for letting me poke around, Sam," Daryll says, still regarding me with that half-smile. "I know you don't care for visitors, so I appreciate you letting me in."

Like I had any choice in the matter. What he means is, *Thanks for not making me kick the fucking door in,* but in a more polite manner.

"Of course," I say, my chest so tight that I fear passing out. He wanders back to the kitchen and grabs the MREs from the counter.

"These are cool to take?"

I nod and try to force a smile. I can't imagine it looks remotely convincing.

"I hope the kid turns up safe." The words come out as a coarse whisper.

"I hope so too."

Daryll leaves my apartment and I lock the door behind him. I fall to my knees and lean my forehead against the door, trying to release the vise on my lungs.

A movie plays out in my head—a low-budget horror movie of a helpless child being torn asunder by an aquatic monster. I see Danny Echols' face, and I can almost taste his blood. But that was just a dream.

***

Panel 1 – The camera faces the barbarian. Blood smears decorate his body, and gore drips from the sword he drags across the coastal sand.

His lips convey a serious, almost stoic expression, but his eyes are filled with passion and desire.

I follow the script and draw what it says. Blue lines come together, forming traps, lats, and triceps. I render waves of wind-blown hair, more suitable for a swimsuit model than a warrior straight out of battle. He grins at me from the paper with perfect teeth, none so much as chipped in any of the hundred battles he's fought.

Thunder strikes outside my apartment as the rain continues to come down. It inspires me to draw a storm into the comic. I fill the background with ominous clouds and bursts of lightning. I scribble sloppy Vs into the skyline—coastal birds fleeing from the storm.

Panel 2 – Focus shifts to the sea witch, a gorgeous, dark-haired woman clad in a sheer robe adorned with skulls and jagged seashells. Her eyes are ancient, over-brimming with the wisdom of ages, while her face holds the stolen youth of a hundred slaughtered virgins.

She makes an arcane gesture with one hand and shouts a threat at our hero. Her expression betrays her lack of confidence, however. There is a measure of fear in her eyes that can't be masked by her gnashing teeth or the smears of black makeup across her face.

As the contours of her body take shape on the page, I realize how much she looks like Aisling. The same wild black hair. The same full lips and dimpled nose. The same alluring air of darkness.

Panel 3 – The barbarian grips the sea witch by the wrist, pulling her toward him. He drags his sword behind him with his other hand. Her free hand forms some semantic gesture and an arcane glow surrounds her slender fingers.

Their faces are only inches apart, and her breasts are pressed tight against his muscled chest. Hate and lust intermingle in their expressions.

I find myself jealous of the barbarian. I'm reluctant to breathe life into him, to give him form and strength with my pencil. He's everything I'm not, and he holds all that I desire.

I do my job, of course. I draw his bulging muscles and his flowing hair. I place the sea witch in his grasp, wishing I had a tenth of his power, cool, and confidence. Imagine what it's like to be fearless. Imagine having the strength to push through every obstacle the world throws at you—to power through the crashing waves of reality that are hellbent on dragging you under.

Panel 4 – Surf crashes on the shore as the barbarian drops his sword and kisses the sea witch. She leans into him, eager for his embrace.

Here I go off script a little. I change the perspective, placing the primary characters in the background as a scrawny figure in a small boat watches them from offshore. He's a no one—an NPC—a disposable extra. His back is turned to the camera, but we see his fists balled tightly at his side, enraged as the display on shore reminds him of his own insignificance.

Panel 5 – The waves crash over the barbarian and the sea witch as they make love on the sand. Keep it PG-13.

I veer from the script again, drawing this as a smaller inset between this panel and the next. The focus is on the sea witch, while I keep the titular brute and his apish muscles off-panel. The witch's eyes are still full of lust, and her mouth expresses the same, but she looks out toward the ocean rather than toward the man atop her. The man in the boat watches in the background, but tentacles seem to be growing out from his torso.

Panel 6 – The script only called for five panels, but I add another. In the foreground we see the scrawny man standing in his boat amid a choppy ocean. Tentacles, like those of an octopus, have erupted from his torso and ripped through his clothes. His back is to the camera, but his attention seems focused on the witch and the barbarian making love on the sand. The stiffness of his posture denotes uneasiness. The tension of his anatomy stands in marked contrast against the fluidity of the alien limbs that wriggle about him.

As I said, the man in the boat is a no one—a piece of window dressing on the stage of the world—or at least he was. He has no name and he's not in the script, but I think he may have a place in the story just yet.

***

The radio says it's Friday. I can only take the broadcaster at her word. One day bleeds into another into another.

She takes some time to talk about the flooding, and I guess it's happening up and down both coasts. Even places like Texas are getting hit hard, and whole landlocked neighborhoods are vanishing beneath waters of the incessant storms.

Much of the information is sparse, and one report often contradicts the next. One thing's for sure: it's at least getting worse here. Looking out the window, it could be half-past noon on a Monday or just after the bars close on a Saturday night. The sky is plastered with storm clouds—a field of non-committal gray that merges with the murky floodwaters at the horizon.

A few days ago I could see the sign for the 7-Eleven on the corner. Now it's lost beneath the surface.

The newscaster hits me with more tragedy and fear-mongering. There is rampant looting and lawlessness around the country. Power grids are down and supply lines are crippled. Hospitals are barely functional. On the plus side, I'm assured that the president and the speaker of the house are both safe, warm, and dry, so I suppose we can all sleep easy now, right?

There is movement beneath the water of the flooded streets. I see foaming wakes and gentle, concentric ripples on the surface. There's something alive out there. Sewer gators, maybe? Are those even real, or is that just a myth? Perhaps it's a group of harbor seals that lost their way? Somehow I think it's something more sinister. That's probably the bad news and the bad dreams intruding upon my imagination though.

I scan the flooded avenue for the Echols boy—the one that went missing from our building—the one who was ripped to bits in my nightmare. I don't know what I'm expecting to see. A scared little boy treading water? The corpse of a child jammed into the doorway of a flooded storefront? There's no one out there.

The woman on the radio begins to share international tragedies, having run out of domestic horrors for the moment. A tanker ship just crashed off the Canadian coast. Governments in Africa and the Middle East are executing people accused of witchcraft. Religious leaders are giving sermons on God's wrath, and eco-nuts are saying that Mother Earth is finally purging herself.

I find myself wondering when things will get back to normal. I find myself wondering *if* things will get back to normal. Will the rain ever stop, or will the water keep rising until it creeps in through the cracks in my windows and consumes me?

I close the curtains and shut off the radio. I'm spiraling, and I need to stop before my last nerve is shot. I need to lie down and calm myself—maybe take a nap. I'm afraid to fall asleep though—afraid that I'll have another one of those terrible dreams—afraid that I'll enjoy it if I do.

I head to my room and drop into bed. The storm taps out a rhythm on my window—a teasing and threatening song to go along with the white flashes of apocalyptic lightning that bleed through the gaps at the sides of my blinds.

I don't think I realized how tired I was. The mattress is soothing, and my anxiety dwindles as sleep overtakes me. The darkness swirls around me, pulling me down. My stiff, achy muscles seem to dissolve into the bedding. I feel fluid and free, but also...

***

...*hungry. I'm so incredibly hungry.*

I crawl out from the dark water and ascend the soggy, carpeted steps. Ambient light from the second-floor windows causes lens flare bursts across my vision. I curse at the light, an inhuman utterance, and keep climbing.

The smell of ammonia overwhelms me, and I become aware of an acute pain that permeates my body. I need to eat, and it needs to be something special. Not another invalid or a half-dead beast, but something rich with life and potential.

Beneath the chemical smell of my failing body, there is the scent of prey. I run my tentacles across the floor and through the air, focusing on that smell...trying to track it. It's close.

The stairs terminate at a long hallway lined with doors on the left and right. I crawl forward, tracking the scent of food. The thing I need lies behind one of these doors.

I run a tentacle along the bottom of apartment 201. The bitter scent of beer and the acrid smell of burning tobacco strike my senses, but nothing that will quell my appetite. The apartment across the hall, 203, stinks of cat piss and chemical air-freshener. The next set of doors, 202 to the left and 205 to the right, hold no promise either—little more than the damp smell of mold that permeates the entire building.

I'm angry and frustrated, but all that goes away as I catch the scent coming from apartment 204—a potpourri of subtle hormones, sweat, and warm milk. I grip the knob, but the door is locked. These apes think themselves clever with their gates and keys, but it will take more than a bit of metal and wood to keep me from my feast.

These apes? Why do I keep thinking of people like that? Why does the thought of the human form invoke such derision in my mind?

I tap on the door, then flatten myself to the ground. My skin changes color, blending in with the darkness and the drab carpeting.

"Hello?" a woman's voice calls from behind the door. "Is someone there?"

I mimic the sound of a child. "Mama..."

"Danny Echols? Is that you, child?"

It occurs to me that she's on the lookout for the missing boy. Daryll would have gone to everyone, asking them to keep an eye out. Is that why I mimicked his voice just now? Was I setting a trap with that knowledge?

The door opens and the woman leans out, glancing back and forth. From my position on the floor, I can barely see her face past her distended belly. It pokes out from under her shirt, beckoning me. I feel like a child staring at a Cadbury Egg on Easter morning.

"Danny?"

I leap upon her, suctioning myself to her skin and encircling her limbs with my own. She gasps, but I cover her mouth before she can scream. A moment later we're falling to the floor as her legs give out beneath my weight.

The tentacle that covers her mouth slithers around her head to cover her nose and eyes. Another limb constricts around her throat, as yet another shuts the door behind us.

I'm urged on by the smell of her pregnancy and the promise of her tender, unborn child. The hormones in her sweat tease my sense of taste and smell—senses that stretch through all of my many limbs. It's quite literally overwhelming, and I fear that my mind can't handle the sensory overload.

The pregnant woman fights back quite fiercely. She reaches out, scrambling for anything she might use as a weapon. Her hand finds a high-heeled shoe, which she begins to pummel me with. The heel doesn't puncture my skin, but it angers me. I grab her wrist and break it. She drops the makeshift weapon, but still claws at me as best she can manage before I pin her arms to the ground. She thrashes and bites at the tentacle around her face, but my skin is too tough and too thick.

Part of me hopes she'll win. I try to scream for her to escape and to run. I try to pull myself off her, but I can't. The good part of me—the human part—is too weak.

Her thrashing slows and her bite weakens. She goes slack and unconscious, but I can feel the baby inside her kicking in panic. I stroke her belly, eager to tear through and devour the little thing inside, but not here...not yet...

***

I wake up choking on vomit, my heart racing. I roll over and retch into my pillow, the taste and smell of the pregnant woman still fresh in my mind.

This wasn't a dream. Neither was the nightmare about Danny Echols. Those things happened. I could feel them. I could smell and taste them. But what about the hentai sex dream with Aisling? That couldn't have been real. Could it?

No, none of it was real. They were all just dreams born from my diseased and anxious mind—the sick, subconscious power fantasies of a pathetic shut-in.

But I can still taste her. I can still smell the child growing in her womb. I can still feel her weakening pulse and her shallow breath.

This wasn't just a dream.

I'm dizzy with contradicting desires and non-sequitur sensations. Fear and confusion dance with hatred and ancient instinct. I'm trembling in my bed, sick to my stomach, but I'm also consumed by hunger; all the while a feeling of religious bliss smolders in the back of my mind. All three feelings are simultaneous, but separate, as if my consciousness is dissolving into other places.

I think of Daryll coming into my home—opening my door and letting the enormous influence of the outside world come crashing in behind him. Did I get caught up in its current? Is it eroding my being and smearing my essence across creation?

Looking into the darkness, I know that there is something out there—some monster dead set on eating a woman and her unborn baby. I know it's not a dream because I can still feel it, and I know just where it's going.

I rise out of bed, wiping the puke from my mouth, and hastily get dressed. Fumbling through my dark apartment, I gather a flashlight and a kitchen knife. I pass my drawing table as I make my way to the door of my apartment. Dead eyes gaze out from my drawing of the fleshy totem. The barbarian stares me down; his gaze is a challenge. He asks, *Are you man enough?*

I nod. It's time to be a hero in lieu of just drawing them. It's time to leave this prison of my own making, and do even one worthwhile thing with my life.

The front door seems to bow as I approach it. The hinges tremble. Wind howls through the hallway on the other side.

I slide the knife under my belt and press my hand against the knob.

"Just open the door..."

What if someone sees me skulking through the halls with a knife? What if they ask what I'm doing? What the hell am I supposed to say to that? I had a dream I was a killer octopus and I'm pretty sure it was real? My throat grows dry just imagining trying to defend myself.

"Just open the door..."

Thunder echoes out in the street and the building shakes. But what if it's not thunder? What if there is something on the other side of this door...something much bigger and meaner than the monster from my dreams? Some kaiju that will break through the walls and drag me out into the floodwaters.

"I can do this..."

I press my head against the door and focus on my breathing. The pressure of all of reality pushes back against the door. The wood pulses beneath my touch, ready to buckle at any moment. I throw up in my mouth even as I tell myself that it's all in my head.

No one is waiting in the halls to catch you sneaking around.

There are no sea monsters waiting to drag you into the flooded streets of Providence.

The entirety of creation isn't going to avalanche upon you once you open this door.

I inhale and steady my body. I exhale and will my heart to slow.

Inhale—I focus on the knots in my stomach.

Exhale—I will the nausea away.

Inhale—I remind myself that I'm in control. Not my fear. Not my anxiety. They don't own me.

Exhale—I open my eyes and steel myself.

"I can do this..."

I throw the deadbolt and grip the knob. The cold touch of the brass sends goosebumps up my arm. Images of monstrous tentacles and hundreds of puckered suction cups invade my mind. I can feel those limbs as surely as I can feel my own twiggy arms.

"Just open the door..."

This time I do.

***

It's dark in the hallway, nearly pitch-black. No light shines in through the window at the far end of the corridor, but wind-driven rain patters against the glass. The only illumination comes in the form of thin slits of light escaping beneath apartment doors.

I switch on my flashlight and shine it toward the floor. The carpet squishes beneath my weight and water squeezes out around the soles of my sneakers. I wonder if the roof is leaking or if the rug is just wicking up the moisture from the flooded ground level. How much black mold hides in these black shadows? My lungs start to burn at the thought, and I find myself stifling a cough.

A flash of lightning bathes the hall in an explosion of white light. For just a moment I can see the waterlogged carpet, the peeling paint of the hallway walls, and the worn apartment doors. The corridor falls dark again in less than a second, but the black seems so much denser now. I swear, even the beam of my flashlight is weaker and more narrow, like its power is being sapped by the shadows. I can feel the dark closing upon me—feel it leaching into my heart.

The wind picks up outside, howling and screaming like a choir of furious specters over the incessant tapping of water on glass. Between the thunder strikes and howling gales, I can hear muffled sounds coming from the other apartments. The cry of a cat. Someone playing an acoustic guitar. An argument between a husband and wife.

The sounds are comforting. They're grounded in the real and mundane—a bit of normality amid the never-ending thunderstorm and the nightmares of tentacled abominations.

I grasp the banister as I make my way down the steps. My knees creak with each step, and I find myself realizing that I haven't walked up or down a flight of stairs in a number of years. I should have started some sort of exercise routine in my hermitage instead of drawing, daydreaming, and watching movies all day.

Halfway down the stairs I find myself winded and hunched over. Is it my weak lungs and out-of-shape body that cause me to gasp for breath as my heart races? Is it the black mold all around me? Or is it my broken mind? All of the above, I suspect.

I focus on my breathing, lean heavily on the railing, and make my way down to the second-floor landing. In the beam of my flashlight, I can see odd tracks on the wet carpet—long, chaotic, crisscrossing indentations. I follow the trail down the hall, straight to apartment 204.

The door is ajar. I knock, then push it open without waiting for an invitation.

"Hello?"

I try to shout, but it only comes out as a whisper. My throat is too tight, my anxiety too great, to produce anything louder.

A single candle sits on the coffee table, lighting up a living room devoid of life. The scent of honeysuckle does little to hide the musty smell of the hall and the stink of whatever food has rotted in the fridge.

I try to call out again, but the words get stuck in my throat. Instead, I step into the apartment. The wet soles of my shoes squeak on the wooden floor. I shine my light at the ground and find damp trails, the same twisting crisscrosses that I had seen on the carpet in the hall.

There is a book lying open on the coffee table—*The Badass Single Mom's Survival Guide*. On the one hand, the book is proof that I'm not a mad man chasing after his dreams. On the other hand, there's a literal fucking monster in the building and I have some kind of connection to it.

I rush out of the apartment and run for the stairwell. Maybe it's some deep well of bravery that I tapped into by finally leaving my apartment. Maybe the bullshit, four-color bravado of the comics I draw has soaked into my soul a bit. All I know is that this woman and her child are in danger, and there's no time to convince anyone else to help them. I'm her only hope, God fucking help us both.

The darkness is almost tangible as I reach the final landing of the stairwell before the flooded first floor. There's a thickness to the air, like how it feels on a humid summer day. Summer is over though, and it isn't hot. There's a chill in the air, and the banister is cold to the touch.

My light catches the surface of the water that has swallowed up the lower steps. The light glitters on the glassy lake—a bloated star left alone to die in a black sea of nothing. The reflection goes supernova as my foot breaks the surface tension and sends out ripples.

By the time I reach the bottom of the stairs, the water is nearly at my chest. I wasn't prepared for how frigid it would be. I can feel the heat being sucked from my body. It's like I'm engulfed in the mist of some gaseous vampire that's draining my life with its touch.

Darkness fills the rest of the space that water does not. I hold my flashlight high and scan for any sign of movement or life. The water is largely still, save for bits of cellophane and cigarette butts floating lazily across the surface. Still, the beam is narrow and weak, allowing only tiny glimpses at a time—the brass number on an apartment door here, a sagging hole in the plaster there. I could easily miss something.

"Hello?"

My voice echoes through the flooded hall, but no one calls back to me. There's no one down here. Maybe I am mad. I suppose it's not entirely unlikely that years in seclusion, coupled with the stress of a natural disaster, might just be too much for my already-fragile psyche.

I laugh to myself—a chuckle of relief that leaves a smile on my face. The prospect of a temporary lapse of reason and a short jaunt into paranoid delusion is certainly preferable to the thought of mind-melding with a sea monster.

As I turn to leave, my flashlight beam catches a glint of metal in the dark. It's a chain lock pulled taut in the gap of a door left ajar. I can't read the number from this angle, but I know what apartment it is.

I trudge toward the partially open door. The flashlight beam jerks erratically as the stress and the cold send tremors through my body. I take deep breaths and try to steady my hand as I point the light at the door. There in the shaky spotlight—a highlighted feature on a pitch-black stage—is the number 107.

This is where I went in my dream—where I took the child. This is where that totem of bone and flesh stood. This is where the monster lives.

I turn off my flashlight and lean into the gap between the door and the frame. The sounds of sloshing and slurping escape the apartment. Something snaps and pops. Something tears. I can hear it all, even above the pounding of my heart. A line from a nature documentary I once watched comes to mind—*the octopus is a messy eater.*

I can't generate enough force to kick in the door, not while I'm submerged up to my chest. Instead, I throw my shoulder into it. The screws holding in the chain lock pull out of the rotted wood on the first try, and I stumble across the threshold.

My head goes under the water as I fall forward, and I'm stricken by just how incredibly cold and dark it is beneath the surface. It's like outer space, but in some distant future when all the stars have been extinguished, or maybe before the first one sparked into existence. It occurs to me that both are the same—past and future aren't linear, but cyclical. What was shall be. What shall be was.

What the hell am I talking about? Why am I waxing pseudo-philosophical as I splash around the depths of a flooded apartment building?

I find my footing and breach the surface. I wipe my eyes and blow the water out from my nose. It's too dark to see, but I can still hear something splashing and eating.

My flashlight won't turn on. Maybe it isn't waterproof. Wouldn't that be a bitch? I smack it a few times and the light flickers on.

The beam is just a sliver, a single golden thread against a tapestry of black. I sweep the light toward the sound, getting little glimpses of the apartment along the way. An antique globe pokes out of the water, all but the northernmost regions of the world lost beneath the flood line. A bookshelf sags under the weight of puffy, waterlogged paperbacks. A tattered poster of Charlie Chaplin barely clings to a wall dotted with black mold. This was someone's life, and just like that, it's been swallowed by the flood and transformed into a den of tragedy.

My light catches movement in the water. The water ripples with pink froth. Why is it pink?

You know why it's pink.

The voice that answers is breathy and feminine—a raspy, whiskey-drenched voice. It belongs to Aisling. I can hear her like she's next to me, but I know she's not. She never is. Still, I take comfort in her voice and I squeeze my hand shut, pretending that I'm holding onto hers.

Don't be afraid to look. It's beautiful... More stunning than the sunrise over India Point... More breathtaking than a meteor shower against the January sky.

"I don't want to see it..." I mutter, afraid of what my flashlight will reveal if I move it even slightly.

When was the last time you saw real beauty with your own eyes?

I can almost feel her breath against my ear.

Not pencil strokes on a page, and not creeping on me through the fisheye lens of your peephole?

I'm afraid to look. I close my eyes to the pink foam on the water. If only I could shut my ears to the sounds of snapping and sloshing.

It's time to see the world as it truly is. You can do this...

She's wrong though. I can't do this.

You can...

What am I even doing down here? I shouldn't be here. I'm not some hero.

Just take one look.

I should be locked away in my apartment. I should be where it's safe and warm.

You can do this... You need to do this.

I open my eyes and shine my light into the corner. The unholy monument sticks out from the water like the ruins of a sunken temple. Dead eyes from a dozen butchered and desecrated creatures stare back at me. Their lifeless eyes burn with malice.

The water splashes and froths in front of the dread totem. There, in the grip of thick, ropy tentacles, I see the corpse of the pregnant woman from apartment 204. Blood runs from the side of her mouth, and the whites of her eyes are blood red. Her arms hang at her side, twisted and broken into unnatural angles. Worst of all is the ragged hole torn into her distended belly. Monstrous limbs probe the red cavern of her torso, scooping out hunks of viscera and tearing the living fetus from her womb.

I told you it was beautiful.

I trudge through the water, screaming for the monster to stop. All I can see are its tentacles. The bulk of it is under the water. I try to fight the thing with all the anger that my crippled mind can muster and all the strength that my feeble body holds. I land a weak blow with the metal flashlight. The monster responds by yanking it away from me and smashing it against the wall.

Now I can't see and I'm all alone with this thing. I swallow hard and wait for it to grab hold of me—for it to drag me under and strip my body for parts for its sinister idol. Several moments pass as I stand with my heart in my throat, but nothing happens.

"Hello?" a voice calls out from the hallway. It's not Aisling. It's not a delusion. It's a real voice, strong and deep—Daryll's voice. "Is somebody in here?"

A flashlight beam cuts through the darkness. It sweeps back and forth, finally landing on me.

"Jesus Christ!" the voice quivers. "What the fuck did you do?"

What did I do? What is he talking about?

"You sick motherfucker, it was you!"

With the spotlight of Daryll's flashlight on me, I can see that the octopus is gone, but the gutted corpse of the woman from 204 bobs on the surface of the water. I stutter and stumble, trying to explain that I didn't do this, that I didn't hurt her, but the words won't come.

Daryll starts forward. I can see his light getting closer. I can hear him sloshing through the water.

I turn toward the sculpture of mortal wreckage. Among the heads and spines of rats and cats, I see the dead face of little Danny Echols staring back at me.

"I swear I didn't..." The words come out a whisper and die in a sob.

The beam of Daryll's light sweeps upward, then back down. I'm so distracted by the movement of the light that I don't even try to dodge his blow. Wild pain erupts in my head and I collapse into the water. The cold blackness doesn't trouble me this time. It feels good, like it's cradling and protecting me. I give into it and find myself alone in the deep...alone in the dark.

***

I melt into the endless ocean. My consciousness thins and spreads through the vast waste, occasionally mingling with the essence of other solute souls. I see with their eyes and hear through their ears. Their anxieties and pangs of hunger flow into me. My neuroses and passions ebb into them.

Purpose and avarice awaken in aquatic beasts like sleeper agents activated by a post-hypnotic phrase. Doomsday prophets sermonize from all ends of the Earth, each shouting their mad ramblings into our shared abyss. Living, breathing gods—not allegorical figures or carved fetishes—proclaim their return, sending tremors through the strings and quarks that make up the cosmos.

I enter the dreams of ancient intelligences and look upon sunken cities and idols strangled by crawling seaweed. Like any dream, the visions shift and change. One moment I'm looking upon a metropolis set in the depths of some alien sea. Towers marked with sharp, bony ridges and riddled with twisting cables stretch high above forests of luminous kelp. The image dissolves and I find myself in the ruins of Dubai, its temples of excess reclaimed by the waters of the Persian Gulf.

My essence passes through the dreamlands of alien tyrants and mingles with the souls of countless beings. I drift into the hazy heroin high of two men shooting dope in a Texas parking lot. I taste the blood of children dragged into the Hudson River. I breathe in loss and grief so profound that it threatens to shatter my mind. I exhale wonder and yearning for beauty that I can't begin to comprehend.

I am everything and nothing—a cell in the body of the universe—a stitch in the fabric of reality.

***

My eyes open, but I'm still alone in the dark. The harsh pain of the physical world presses upon me. Agony pulses through my head in time with inarticulate, arrhythmic howls of rage. A monstrous voice, vaguely feminine, demands my blood. She calls me a pervert, a bastard, and a devil.

In the space between her screeches and sobs, I can hear muffled responses. A masculine voice tries to calm her. Another woman says something about the police. I try to listen, but it's hard to make out much of anything.

A strip of duct tape holds a gag in my mouth. I don't know where I am, but it's a small space and I'm curled into a ball. A closet, perhaps? I try to stand but find that I'm bound at the ankles and wrists. The cord bites into my skin as I struggle to free myself, and I gasp in pain.

It's no use struggling. I'm not strong enough. If only I were like the heroes I drew, I could burst free. If only I were like the monsters I dreamed of, I could slither loose. But I'm not like either. I'm weak and stiff and afraid.

The scornful howls cease and are replaced by breathy sobs. It's easier to hear the others now. They're talking about the thing in the basement: not the monster, but the idol of carnage that it fashioned.

"Ms. Echols is right, we need to deal with him." I don't recognize the voice. "No fucking jury would ever convict us."

"Do we know it was him for sure?" a woman argues. "He could have just stumbled upon it."

"I've been here two years and that dude has never left his unit once," another stranger responds. "No way he just decided to go for a stroll to the flooded-out first floor."

"Wayne's right." It's Daryll talking now, but I have no clue who Wayne is. "I was in his apartment. He had a drawing of that nightmare on his desk. It's some sick fucking art project."

A loud moan silences everyone, then fades into more quiet sobbing.

"Will someone get her a Valium or something?"

"I still think we should call the police."

"With what fucking phone, genius?"

"Enough!" Daryll shouts. Everyone goes silent. "We'll put it to a vote."

They all mumble over one another, but their tone sounds agreeable. My fate is going to be decided by a fucking committee meeting—by neighbors who think I'm a depraved lunatic shut-in.

"Who thinks we should keep him tied up and wait for the cops?"

There are a few soft ayes. The grieving woman—Ms. Echols, I assume—begins screaming at them.

"You fucking cowards! You pieces of shit! He killed my baby!"

A chorus of hushed voices erupts in response. Daryll tries to calm everyone, then asks who votes for them to "take care of it" themselves.

This option gets a more vocal and enthusiastic response than calling the police.

A brief argument ensues. I hear a few people protest the decision. They call it criminal. They say they won't be party to such a thing. I pray that their reason and conscience will spread, or that they'll do something to stop the others. Instead, they leave, washing their hands of the whole mess like Pilate.

With the dissenters gone, my remaining neighbors debate over who will serve as my executioner. Ms. Echols volunteers. She practically begs to do the deed. The others don't dare deny her. I suppose I wouldn't either, if the roles were reversed.

The door opens, and the glow of a camping lantern invades the darkness of my closet-prison. I tremble on the floor, looking up at the people who mean to take my life. If only I could speak and defend myself. If only I could tell them the truth.

It doesn't matter. What good would the truth be, even if I could speak it?

This is all a misunderstanding. I was framed by a giant, psychic octopus.

Daryll steps into the doorway, eclipsing the light with his mass. He grips my collar and drags me from the closet. I find myself in some stranger's bedroom.

Neighbors I've never met—a merciless jury—form a half-circle around me. Their glares are hateful and dumb. The storm rages outside, battering the windows with wind and rain, adding a deeper layer of theatricality to the terrible scene.

Daryll forces me to my knees and I look each of my accusers in the face. I only recognize a few of them. Ms. Echols, whose name I never knew before her boy went missing. Daryll, of course, and a few others I've caught glimpses of from my window as they come and go.

Behind them all stands Aisling. I feel my heart begin to break at the thought of her hating me—of her thinking me a deranged killer.

Ms. Echols approaches me. A tear rolls from her cheek and lands on the aerated blade of the steak knife in her hand. The reality of the situation strikes me. I'm going to die, here and now, murdered for a crime I had no part in.

I never should have opened my door. I never should have left my apartment. I never should have tried to be a hero.

Ms. Echols kneels so we can be face to face. I have never seen an expression of such derision before. She runs the edge of the blade down my cheek, taking bitter pleasure as I wince.

Whispers erupt from my neighbors, a mixture of protests and approval. I look from one to the next, pleading with only my eyes, silently begging someone to intervene. Some look away. Others return my gaze with cold stoicism.

"Don't you look at them," Ms. Echols mutters, nudging my face back toward hers with the flat of her blade. "They can't save you, you fucking monster. If Jesus, Moses, and Muhammed strolled in right now, they couldn't save you."

I can hear the tapping of water droplets bleeding through window sashes and pooling on the frames. The outside world is forcing itself in. It's about to overtake me. It's about to crash over all of us.

"You took him... You ruined my sweet little boy." Her words are broken by moans and sobs as she presses the serrated edge of the steak knife beneath my earlobe. "Now I'm going to ruin you."

Robbed of my voice, I shake my head back and forth. She presses a finger to my lips, shushing me, and nods yes.

"Jesus Christ, man," one of the neighbors who condemned me to death exclaims. "This is sick. Does she really need to torture him? Can't we just put a bullet in his head?"

"You didn't see the thing downstairs," Daryll answers. "He killed a child and a pregnant woman. He deserves whatever she gives him."

This isn't fair. I didn't hurt anyone. I've never hurt anyone.

Didn't you?

It's Aisling's voice, not out loud, but in my head...a figment of my imagination, the same as always.

You shared Samael's flesh as he dragged the simple little bastard to the basement. You felt the boy's bones snap and you tasted his marrow.

I shift my eyes and catch Aisling's gaze. She stands behind the rest of the mob, a playful smirk on her lips. She raises her eyebrows in a teasing gesture, as if she and I share an amusing secret that the others aren't privy to.

I'm reading into it...projecting a connection where there is none. We don't have some supernatural connection. She's not speaking directly into my mind.

Yes, I am.

I'm broken and desperate, that's all.

Broken, desperate, and beautiful. I only wish I knew you earlier. We could have had such times. We still—

Aisling's voice cuts out as agony lights up my neurons like Times Square. The gag muffles my screams as Ms. Echols saws through the webby tissue of my earlobe and into the cartilage. I squirm and flinch, but it only causes the skin to tear.

I can help, if you want.

"Yes!" I try to scream through the gag and the duct tape, but it comes out as an inarticulate moan. Ms. Echols is in my face, cutting and cursing, blocking my view of Aisling. If only I could see her—if only I could see if my plea for help registered on her face, or if I'm just a lunatic.

What if I did kill those people and build that abomination? I'm hearing voices and having violent dreams. Could I be crazier than I thought? Not just an agoraphobic mess, but a delusional psychopath?

Blood pools into my ear canal and Ms. Echols keeps cutting, hellbent on dismembering me before I die. She cries and screams, barraging me with spit and foul breath. She bellows about how much pain she's going to inflict on me, and I believe her.

I close my eyes and imagine Aisling's gorgeous face. I silently beg her to save me, knowing the whole time how stupid and insane I am.

All you had to do was ask.

The knife gets stuck in a bit of cartilage, and I nearly vomit from the pain as Ms. Echols yanks the blade free. She flicks the blood from the knife like some dime-store samurai. I get the ludicrous idea that I should remember her movements and body language so that I can mimic it in a drawing someday.

Ms. Echols pulls the flap of my ear away from my skull. She slides the knife into the wound and within three strokes separates my ear from my head.

Blindness and vertigo, born of pain and trauma, overtake me. Nothing but suffering exists for several heartbeats. I weep with my head bowed as Ms. Echols hurls insults and grim promises at me.

There is no hope. I'm going to die here, and then they'll throw my corpse into the floodwaters—into the deep and dark.

My nose twitches at the stink of ammonia. Before I can make sense of it, all hell breaks loose. There's a crash, then a scream, and everyone, including Ms. Echols, turns toward the commotion. I follow their gazes and stare dumbfounded at the impossible scene before me.

One of my vigilante neighbors—a middle-aged man with a slight paunch—seems to be flying. His body, barely visible in the shadowed corner of the room, slides up the wall and toward the ceiling. There is no grace to his ascent. He flails like a kite caught in a hurricane, and his cries are the dying wails of a Hollywood scream queen.

His body spins mid-air, and he slams face-first into the ceiling, not once or twice, but three times in succession. Blood erupts from his broken nose, leaving a crimson Jackson Pollock spatter above us. He falls and levitates a foot away from the ceiling. Blood spreads across his face, like a comic book symbiote masking his human features.

Daryll picks up the lantern and holds it up toward the limp, floating man. The light spreads across the ceiling and I can see it now—a mass of tentacles converging at a bulbous center.

The monster is almost invisible, its mottled skin nearly the same shade of white as the textured ceiling. One of its terrible limbs is curled around the waist of my lifeless neighbor. He's not flying; the beast is holding him aloft.

The octopus tightens its grip, crushing the man's waist like a hydraulic girdle. Bones snap and organs pop. Blood pours from every orifice. I'm reminded of a tube of toothpaste being squeezed by an overzealous child.

My neighbors scream and rush for the door. Before they can make it, the monster snatches the light from Daryll's hand. The lantern crunches in its grip and the room goes dark. I hear the door slam shut at the same moment. It all happens too fast for anyone to escape.

The next few moments are defined by echoing cries and the spray of warm blood. Flashes of lightning reveal horror movie snapshots. Limbs are torn from sockets. Spines and ribs break against walls of plaster and lathe. Tentacles strike like living scourges.

This is no comic book. There's no fighting back—no epic battle. Ms. Echols, for all her righteous anger, is torn in half and discarded before me. Her rage and her grief are reduced to nothing.

The others fall just as easily. Their fates are just as grim. Even Daryll, his brawn so much like the heroes I draw, is like a rag doll to the beast. It picks him up like a toy and batters him against the walls and the ceiling, pulverizing his innards and crushing his skull.

The madness ceases as quickly as it began. The screams and the sounds of violence are replaced with quiet labored breaths, the pattering of raindrops against the window, and the rhythmic dripping of blood from ruined corpses.

I look for Aisling's body among the dead, but it's too dark to see except in those brief moments when lightning flashes. Still, I try to make out a pale arm decorated with swirls of black ink, or a porcelain face smeared with dark makeup. If she's here, I don't see her.

The creature drops its camouflage, revealing a skin tone like patinated copper. Its emerald flesh takes on a glow and bathes the room in eldritch light. Invisible only moments ago, the creature is now impossible to miss. The beast is as big as a man—larger, perhaps. It saunters through the room, its movements so fluid and strange.

I wait for it to strike at me—to rip me to pieces and use my dismembered body for its unholy sculpture down on the first floor. To my surprise, the octopus ignores me and gathers up bits of my neighbors.

A ghostly woman steps into the room, her ebony dress a midnight umbra against the dark backdrop. Her skin is the color of moonlight, and she walks through the carnage with the same detached grace as the monster. She strokes one of the creature's writhing limbs as she walks by it.

"Don't worry," Aisling's voice calls out. "They, too, are broken and beautiful now, but it's only skin deep."

She kneels beside me, tears the duct tape from my lips, and pulls the gag out of my mouth.

"You and I, we're beautiful where it counts..." She presses her mouth to my forehead. Her kiss is warm and wet. "And we are broken where it counts."

Aisling leans back and places one finger beneath my chin. She nudges my head up so that our eyes meet. My heart races and my dick swells, despite the abhorrent circumstances and the incredible pain I'm in. I've obsessed over her for so long—fantasized about touching and tasting her—dreamed of my name on her lips. Now she is inches away, her breath on my face.

In the monster's outré glow, I note the minutiae of her flesh—the inconsistent shading of her tattoos, the raised razor-scar slivers on her arms and chest, and the laugh lines that stretch out beyond her thick eyeliner. Each nuance accentuates her beauty more deeply.

She pulls a blade from her boot: not some delicate Ren Faire weapon made for show, but a cheap box cutter. She clicks it open, a wicked smile on her face.

"Please don't kill me." I cringe at the quiver in my voice.

She grabs me by the hair and throws me to the floor. I land on my face, the rough carpet scratching at my forehead.

I wait for the sting of her blade across my throat and for the warm wash of my own blood down my chest. Instead, I'm met with but a nick on the back of my wrist as she cuts my bonds.

"We're not here to die...not just yet. We're here to bear witness."

The massive octopus drags the wreckage of my neighbors behind it as it exits the apartment. Their severed heads and ruined faces stare at me with lifeless eyes and static expressions of pain. Even in death, they gaze upon me with crushing judgment.

"You're an artist, Sam. Aren't you curious about Samael's process? It's beautiful to watch." There's no irony or sadism in Aisling's voice as she speaks. She's sincerely enamored with this thing and its perverse sculpture.

"It...it just killed everyone, Aisling."

"I see," she says with a frown. "You're not ready yet, but you will be."

She turns and follows the fading glow of the retreating beast she calls Samael.

"You're not thinking right!" I call after her. "That thing... It's gotten into your head! It's in both of our heads!"

She doesn't turn back. She doesn't reply. I find myself alone again in the dark, left with nothing but the stink of spilled viscera and the sound of the hungry storm as it devours the city.

***

PAGE ONE –

Panel 1 – Weak sunlight from an overcast sky barely penetrates Sam's apartment. Covered in blood and filth, he hesitates at the door, gripping the frame with one hand. His other arm hangs at his side, a shotgun dangling in his grip. His eyes are closed, and an expression of conflict is written across his face.

CAPTION: I can do this...

Panel 2 – Close up of Sam's hand as he turns the doorknob. His fingers leave streaks of gore on the brass.

CAPTION: Just open the door...

Panel 3 – The camera is looking at Sam from behind. He's opened the door and is framed in its center—a dark figure against a deeper black. The knob and the doorframe have bloody handprints from where he touched them. The hallway beyond is a void.

CAPTION: I can do this...

Panel 4 – Sam steps into the hall, his shotgun held at the ready. The darkness swallows him. He's barely visible, just enough for the reader to make him out.

CAPTION: I'm no hero... No soldier or badass. But there's no one else left to save her.

Panel 5 – Sam approaches the stairwell leading to the lower floors of the building. We see a flash of lightning through a window over the stairs. White light washes over the scene, exposing crumbling plaster and casting wild shadows across the walls. Sam's own shadow is the dominant image of the panel. Twisting black tendrils extend out from its otherwise human shape.

CAPTION: I know that the beast is inside me, just as it's in her. I can feel it twisting my mind and tainting my soul.

PAGE TWO –

Panel 1 – An octopus, the size of a man, glides through the dark water of a flooded apartment building. The creature gives off a slight glow, making it visible to the reader. There's a dance-like litheness to its movements. Its body is all strength and grace.

CAPTION: But this connection, it's a two-way street. I'm inside it as well.

Panel 2 – An idol of dead flesh rises above the water line in a flooded apartment. It's a nightmarish thing cobbled together from lifeless faces and scraps of flesh and fur. The expressions on the severed heads and the angles of the broken limbs jutting out from the mass are a testament to suffering and madness.

Aisling stands before the idol, her naked breasts just above the waterline. Her arms are raised in a V as she praises and worships the monstrosity.

CAPTION: I know where it lives. I know where it eats. I know where it performs its profane rites.

Panel 3 – Close-up of Aisling's face. Her eyes are pure white behind the smears of black makeup surrounding them. Her expression is both mad and ecstatic.

CAPTION: I know what it has done to my lover... How it has conquered her will and how it holds her in thrall.

Panel 4 – The monstrous octopus rises from the water and embraces Aisling with its many limbs. Her flesh glows in its bioluminescence. She throws her head back and bites her lip at its wretched touch.

CAPTION: I have felt it defile both her soul and her flesh.

Panel 5 – A hole explodes in the center of the octopus. One of its limbs is blown off. Aisling screams out in shock as it sprays green ichor across her face and chest.

CAPTION: And I'll be damned if I let it happen again.

AISLING: Ahhh!

SFX (OFF-PANEL SHOTGUN): Boom!

PAGE THREE –

Splash Page – Sam stands in the waist-high water, holding a smoking shotgun. His face is an angry snarl with a dash of cool, somewhere between Clint Eastwood in *Dirty Harry* and Nic Cage toward the end of *Mandy*.

SAM: ~~Sorry, asshole, but your princess is in another castle.~~

~~Get your filthy tentacles off my lady!~~

~~Sorry, was I interrupting something?~~

(Maybe I should keep this page silent. It might be more dramatic without a dumb one-liner.)

47

I keep drawing, dedicating my fantasies to the page as if that will make them real. The next five panels depict me blowing holes through the monster with my limitless-ammo Mossberg. We have a few images of Aisling awakening from its spell—her pupils returning and her ecstasy decaying into fright. It's all very dramatic.

Next is another splash page. She falls into my embrace as we kiss in the filthy depths of the flooded apartment. It's cathartic, I suppose, but it's all bullshit.

I'd hoped if I could visualize it... If I could draw it all out...then maybe I'd have the balls to take Samael on in some action-movie showdown. That's not who I am though.

That thing crumpled up Daryll like he was a paper doll. It's practically invisible and moves like fucking lightning. Even if I wasn't a neurotic pussy...even if I had a gun and knew how to use it...even if ad fucking infinitum... Well, I'd stand about as much of a chance against this thing as Lloyd Kaufman stands of getting an Oscar.

I'm not some comic book barbarian. I'm not Arnold Schwarzenegger in *Predator*. Hell, I'm not even Danny Glover in *Predator 2*.

Maybe I don't have to be. Who the fuck says I have to fight this thing to win? No, I just need to convince Aisling to run with me. We'll take off and get far away from this charnel house and the demon stalking the halls. And if she refuses, then I'll leave on my own.

Yes, we'll run...but where to? Out into the hungry waters beneath the crumbling sky? Outside where the world waits to fall upon me like an avalanche?

I look up from my drawing table and glance out the window. I think it's daytime; at least, it's brighter than it has been in a while. The water level is higher, and I fear the ocean and the storm may just swallow all of Providence.

The canals that once were streets seem to stretch right on into the Atlantic. I can almost feel the undertow pulling me at me—threatening to drag me out into the vast and churning sea. I shudder at the thought of the sky flaying me with hail and wind as the ocean batters me this way and that, each force of nature hungry for a piece of my death.

The monster could have killed me several times, yet it hasn't. Is it any safer out in the flooded city? And can I even bring myself to wade out into the world? I haven't left this building in years. What makes me think I'll be able to stroll out beneath the crushing weight of the sea and the sky?

I can do this...

***

The door to Aisling's apartment is ajar. I knock before entering and call out her name, but there's no answer. The door creaks as I step across the threshold, and deeper in the apartment I hear quiet singing.

A dozen noxious smells assault me as I enter Aisling's living room. The scents of ash and tobacco mingle with the sweet stench of rotten food and the boozy smell of cheap wine. Below it all is the lingering smell of ammonia. I always imagined her place smelling different, like cloves and burning leaves.

Black drapes are pulled to either side of the windows, and gray light streams in. The floor is covered in trash and debris. Dirty dishes litter every surface, and each plate and cup holds a dozen cigarette butts.

Macabre decorations cover the walls—photographs of serial killers and rock stars, ugly paintings of violent sex, and taxidermy bats mounted in wooden boxes. One wall is lined with books and graphic novels. Some of them I recognize—Alan Moore's *From Hell*, *Wytches* by Snyder and Jock, a whole row of Stephen King doorstoppers. Most of them are more obscure, or at least outside of my spheres of interest—*Enochian Magic for Beginners*_by Donald Tyson, *Misery Obscura* by Eerie Von, *The Primal Screamer* from Nick Blinko.

"Aisling?" She ignores me and keeps singing to herself in some other room.

My eyes land on the remnants of a shattered aquarium that sits on a table in the corner. The wooden floor beneath the table is warped and discolored from water damage. Shards of broken glass cover the floor and hang from the metal frame of the tank.

A tiny haunted house sits on a bed of neon-blue pebbles inside the remnants of the aquarium. A miniature mailbox, the kind that sits on a post in the suburbs, pokes up in front of the house. The name *Samael* is scrawled on the side of the mailbox.

"It wasn't so long ago that he could fit in there." Aisling's voice is soft and her tone is warm, but I jump at the sound. "God, how he has grown."

I turn to find her standing in the doorway to her bedroom. Gore from the slaughter of neighbors has crusted in her hair. Her bare thighs, painted in rust-colored streaks of dried blood, poke out from beneath an oversized sweatshirt, and I find myself wondering if she's wearing anything beneath. What a ridiculous, lonely man I am, for my mind to go there in a time like this.

"Don't beat yourself up, Sam," she says as if she can read my thoughts. "You've been alone for such a long time. It's only natural."

She holds her hand out and takes a step back into her bedroom. I want to follow her. I want to touch her and taste her. I want to be inside her and feel her wrapped around me.

"There isn't much time left, Sam. If you want something, you should take it."

I close my eyes and suck in a deep breath.

"This is all wrong, Aisling. We need to get away from here... Away from that thing."

"There is no getting away, Sam. You, and I, and Samael... We're all part of something so much bigger now."

Her beauty, her voice, the gravity of her soul and mind—these things dig into me like fishhooks. They pierce my being and threaten to drag me into madness and oblivion. But dare I tear myself away? Can I take that kind of pain?

"I wish I could have loved you...for real, not just in my mind." A tear runs down my face, cutting through the crusted blood of my neighbors. "Goodbye, Aisling."

***

I stand in the flooded lobby of my apartment building. The water is deeper now, nearly to my neck. The door hangs open on sagging hinges, letting in the wind and the rain.

I trudge through the water and place my hand against the door frame. The paint crumbles at my touch and the wood beneath is soft.

Looking out into the drowned city, I see a million tiny horrors. A crow sits atop a corpse that floats across the water. The bird picks at the dead man's swollen flesh. Prescription bottles float like tiny buoys, their chemical contents incapable of holding back the tide of madness that's sweeping over the world. White ripples upset the water's surface, hinting at living nightmares just below.

"I can do this..."

Lightning strikes somewhere in the distance, but the light barely brightens the storm clouds. The sky is so heavy—so dense—that it's only a matter of time before it collapses upon us. My chest tightens as I imagine being buried beneath the weight of the storm-choked heavens.

"I can do this..."

The water tugs at my feet, urging me into the canals and out to the endless sea. The winds scream in hunger, eager to feed upon my flesh and soul. The titanic beast called Providence waits just beyond this threshold, ready to grind me in its concrete teeth.

"I... I can't do this."

***

I find Aisling standing naked in front of the window when I come back to her apartment. She's singing to herself again, and staring out into the storm.

"I knew you'd come around," Aisling says without turning to greet me.

I walk over to her and place my hands on her hips. She leans back against me, and I hold her as I've dreamed to so many times.

"There's nothing out there but death," I say.

"There's nothing anywhere but death, at least for our kind." She takes my hand and gives it a gentle squeeze. "But you and I, we get to bear witness at least."

"Bear witness to what?"

"The end. The beginning. It's all the same, depending on how you choose to see it."

"I don't understand what's happening."

"We aren't meant to, not fully. Our brains are too small and primal. But that doesn't mean we can't appreciate the beauty of it."

Aisling strips off my wet clothes and leads me to her bed. She pushes me down onto the blood-stained sheets and climbs onto me. Caught in the hypnotic gaze of her emerald eyes, I realize that there's nothing I want more than her touch. Let the world drown. Let the sky fall. It's worth it to be in her bed.

She guides me inside her and we moan in unison. It's been years since I've been touched in this way...years since I've known any kind of intimacy.

She drives down against my hips. Her dark, filthy hair teases my face as she leans down to kiss me. Our lips touch and my mind is flooded with knowledge that my simian brain can't process—the histories of races that were ancient when our sun was young—forbidden geometries that can open secret passages in the fabric of the cosmos—yearnings and hungers that make the deepest human passion seem as shallow and sterile as elevator music.

The sum of all reality crashes over me like a tidal wave, just as I've feared it would for all these years. I can't fight anymore. I can't run. Instead, I admire its enormous grandeur—the maddening ocean of eternity. I know that it will crush me—that it will dash me on the rocks and dissolve my soul—but that's okay. I'm no longer afraid.

THE INNSMOUTH LOOK

Brett J. Talley

THE DAY AFTER the world ended, I received an invitation to a gala ball. When the letter arrived, I was, like most people who still had power, watching the reports of a large chunk of Europa that had smashed into the Ross Ice Shelf. We didn't know it was Europa at the time. That information would come later, when what was left of the scientific community were able to piece together the sequence of events that tolled the bell on our civilization. Not that it mattered. Whether it was an asteroid or a meteor or a meteorite or a rogue chunk of Jupiter's moon—whatever the newscaster decided to call it—the consequences were the same. The reception was spotty with the fried satellites, massive coastal flooding, and torrential rain that followed. But it was hard to miss the mentions of an "extinction level event."

Needless to say, I was not expecting the mail would run that day.

And, in fact, it didn't. The letter was delivered by a 20-something on a motor scooter, drenched under his helmet and flimsy jacket. I gave him a large tip and took the soaking envelope into my apartment. There was no return address. Inside was a letter, handwritten. It read:

Mr. Beckett,

The presence of your company is requested at a small gathering at the estate of Falwell Somerson this Tuesday at 7 PM. No RSVP is required.

The letter was unsigned. In ordinary times, I would have avoided such a gathering. Doubtless, Somerson and his crew were not my people, and cocktail parties have never been my scene. But a party at the end of time was something I didn't think I could miss. So I dug out my best suit, found some old dress shoes, and began to practice my elocution.

Somerson's estate was on several hundred acres outside of town. His mansion sat on the only significant rise for miles, an imposing fortress ruling over the rolling plains that surrounded it. As I drove through the rain, I thought it lucky for Somerson that his home might be the only one in the area to survive the inevitable floods that were coming. An island of ruined wealth in a sea of misery, an Ozymandias for our age.

The "small gathering" turned out to be quite a party, and I was forced to park far enough away that I was sopping wet by the time I reached the front door. The large man who answered didn't seem to mind. He had already grown accustomed to our new, soggier environment.

"Do you have a mask?" he asked.

"A mask?" I said as I handed him my soaking overcoat. The pandemic had ended years before, and infection seemed as if it should be the last of our concerns.

"This is a masquerade ball," he said matter-of-factly.

"Oh," I said, blushing. "*That* kind of mask. Well, no, I don't."

The man snorted as if he were deeply disappointed in me. He opened a cabinet and removed a mask in the classic style of Venice. Apparently, I was not the only one to forget or, more accurately, to be failed to be informed, for it was one of many. This mask was pure white, one of those plague doctor things that looks like a bird's beak. I took it and slipped it over my face. Only then did the man step aside.

Were it not for what was going on in the world, I'd still say that the scene that opened before me was bizarre. Men and women, masked and holding champagne, drinking and dancing and laughing. There's a type of person for whom that might sound magical. But not me. And indeed, the sound of the classical music from the miniature symphony could only just mask the sound of raindrops pelting against the ceiling-high windows. My mind drifted back a couple decades, to an English class in a crumbling high school that had been demolished the year after I'd graduated. We'd read "The Masque of the Red Death" by Edgar Allen Poe. How silly, I'd thought. What an unrealistic story. And yet here I stood, waiting for my own personal Prospero to announce the purpose of this gathering.

I hadn't been there long when the man from the door tapped me on the shoulder.

"Mr. Somerson would like to see you."

I followed the man down a long hallway to a set of double doors. He opened them to one of those libraries you see in movies but that I didn't believe existed in real life. The kind with two stories of books and a giant globe in the center that likely contained thousands of dollars' worth of scotch. Somerson was standing beside it, glass already in hand. He glanced up as I entered, and looked at me with a smile that reached his eyes.

"Ah, Mr. Beckett. I'm pleased to finally make your acquaintance."

I could tell he meant it as he gestured for me to join him at the globe. And yet, though I did not doubt his sincerity, I wondered at it anyway. I couldn't imagine why a man like Somerson would have any interest in meeting a man like me.

"Would you like one?" he asked, raising the ice-filled glass in his hand.

"Sure," I said. "But make mine neat."

Somerson nodded to the ogre still standing over my shoulder. I glanced backward as I heard him leave.

"I suppose," Somerson said, "that we'll need an update on this soon." He spun the globe casually with his free hand. "In the old days, there wasn't a job more important, or more dangerous, than cartography. The mapmakers who traveled the world, who made the continents what they are, gave them their shape. There hasn't been much need for them for the last century or so. But with most of the satellites gone or out of commission, I have a feeling they will be back in demand. New coasts to map. New harbors to explore."

"You make it sound almost romantic."

"What's the old saying? When life hands you lemons?"

Somerson poured a glass of scotch as he spoke, somber smile fading from his face. He handed it to me, bowing slightly.

"Some might say the end of the world is a little more than some lemons."

"Perhaps. But I hold to the long view of things. The world never ends, Mr. Beckett. When the meteorite struck that killed the dinosaurs, the world didn't end. Only changed. Made new again, for the coming of man."

"I doubt that made the dinosaurs feel any better about the situation."

"True," he said, chuckling, "very true. And that, I suppose, is why I have brought you here tonight. What if I told you that it didn't have to be the end? What if I told you the world could be saved?"

"That would be a pretty interesting thing to hear, Mr. Somerson. But I can't imagine what it would have to do with me."

He spun the globe again, then tilted it and pointed at the south pole. "Forty-eight hours ago, something struck here, on the Ross Ice Shelf. The popular consensus is that it was a meteor, perhaps a dead comet. The truth is that it was a piece of a moon."

"A piece of the moon hit us?"

"Not *the* moon, Mr. Beckett. A moon. Europa, one of Jupiter's moons, one of the few places in the known galaxy that might support life."

"You're going to tell me aliens from Jupiter did this?"

He chuckled. "Not quite. And yet, in a way. No, Mr. Beckett, I am telling you that a few months ago, there was a meteor strike on that moon, one that dislodged...well...something. Something that then traveled several million miles to strike here, in the center of the Ross Ice Shelf. This is not speculation. It is a fact, I can assure you. And that fact is why half the eastern seaboard is either under water or well on its way, with more surely to follow. It's the reason it is raining tonight, and will probably rain every night for many nights to come. It is the reason that our civilization's continued existence is now a questionable prospect."

"That's all very interesting, Mr. Somerson, but I'm still not sure what it has to do with me."

The old man grinned. "Your reputation precedes you, Mr. Beckett. The authorities never did find that Van Gogh that managed to walk itself out of the Boston Museum of Art, did they?"

"They did not," I said. It made sense now. Somerson wanted something somebody wasn't willing to sell, and he figured what better time to get it than the middle of an apocalypse. I'd had some friends who had similar ideas. Security was no longer at the top of most people's priority list. There was a simple reason for that. You save for a rainy day with the expectation that the sun will come out eventually. It was certainly raining now, but there weren't many sunny days on the horizon.

"I won't say I'm not intrigued, Mr. Somerson. But I'd be lying if I said business was a priority right now. My plans are to get as far inland as I can. Maybe find a nice mountain top to wait this one out. Unless you are offering to help with that, I'm afraid I'm going to have to refuse whatever offer you want to make."

Most of my clients are people who aren't used to hearing no, and when they do, they tend to get upset. I expected the same from Somerson. Instead, as we stood there in that darkened library, the rain hammering on the windows and the sound of laughter echoing in from the rooms beyond, Somerson merely smiled. But there was no joy in it. Only sadness.

"I wish it were as simple as that, Mr. Beckett, but I don't think you understand. This," he said, gesturing toward the windows, "this isn't just the unfortunate effects of an entirely unpredictable disaster. It's something so much more than that. There are forces that move beyond our sight, and they have conspired to change this world to make it more to their liking. Much damage is done already, yes, but there is so much more to come. That we can stop. If we act now."

Nothing about Somerson led me to believe he was insane. He was, in fact, perfectly lucid. But the words he was telling me now would have been appropriate in the ravings of a crazed lunatic. That he believed what he was saying was evident; that I needed to get out of there, clear.

"Mr. Somerson..."

He stopped me with a raised hand. "You don't have to believe me. It's not important. You can think me crazy if you like. It's no matter. Do what I ask and I will transfer $10 million into the bank account of your choice. And it just so happens I have property in Nebraska, near Omaha, as far from the sea as you can hope to get. It's yours if you do this one thing for me."

I frowned. The world might be screwed, but $10 million is $10 million. I looked down at the globe, and in my mind I could almost see the oceans rise, the cities flood, the country drown. What the hell. "Okay. You have a deal. What do you need me to do?"

"I need you to retrieve a book for me."

"A book? That's it?"

"It's not just any book."

"It never is."

"Do you know of Miskatonic University?"

There was no one in my game who didn't know of Miskatonic University. When you deal in rare and unusual artifacts, you quickly learn where the most valuable ones are located. And yet, I'd never known anyone to make any attempt at...liberating...those artifacts from the university. There were too many rumors, too many secrets, too many stories about men who went into the vaults at Miskatonic and never came out. I'm not superstitious. You can't be to do this work. But unlike the curse of the Pharaohs or the magic of the Mayans, whatever haunted the halls of Miskatonic was real. And it was to be feared.

"I've heard of it. Can't say I've ever been there."

He smiled. "No, if you'd been there, I imagine you wouldn't be here. But you're also the only person I know of who has the, how should I put it, confidence to recover something from that place for me."

"Confidence. That's one word to use."

"Miskatonic has many treasures, of course, but there is only one that interests me, only one that might be capable of ending this madness. It is the *Incendium Maleficarum*, and I must have it."

The *Incendium Maleficarum*. My God, he *was* crazy. The tales told about that ancient book were enough to send shivers down the strongest spines. If the book even existed, and I had long doubted it did, that Miskatonic should have it seemed impossible to imagine. I'd been asked to find it before, but my investigations had always hit a dead end of mist and mystery.

"You doubt me?" he asked, apparently catching the look of utter shock on my face. "You think it a myth? It is not. I have spent the better part of my life researching it, tracking its path through the centuries, all the way to Miskatonic. I spent the rest of my time accumulating the wealth I needed to acquire it. But, alas, when men make plans, the gods laugh."

"And so here we are."

"Here we are."

"So, what, you want me to get the book so you can read it as the world ends?"

"No, I want to *stop* the world from ending. And with that book, I can do it. You don't have to believe me, Mr. Beckett. Just bring me the book. You'll receive your reward. And whatever will be will be. I can assure you, if I fail, it will make things no worse than they already are. Do we have an agreement?"

He stood and offered his hand. I'd already decided a few things. One, he was definitely crazy. Two, I didn't care. Three, he was right. What did I have to lose? I took his hand, and we had a deal.

"I can't make any promises, but I'll go to Miskatonic and see what I can find."

"Just know this, Mr. Beckett. You won't be the only one looking."

***

I left for Massachusetts the next morning. The rain had not let up, and there was no indication it would. I spun the radio through the FM dial and picked up nothing but static. A few AM stations still came through, but it was all the same message: the end is nigh. I didn't need a preacher to tell me that. Despite the rain, the drive was easy. There weren't many folks heading toward the coast. The westbound lanes, on the other hand, were full. People had packed everything they had into their overfilled cars and headed to what they hoped was drier land. Every inch of space was taken, and bags were stacked on top to soak in the rain.

But it was the other cars that bothered me more, the ones parked on the shoulder or in the median or nose-first in a ditch. Doors open, things left behind, but people gone. I wondered what happened to them, where they went in the endless rain.

Rivers rose and bridges struggled under the strain. The windshield wipers beat a steady tattoo, but even at their highest speed I had to imagine the road as much as see it in front of me. I drove like that for hours, crossing over state line after state line until Massachusetts loomed before me. I took the interstate till the Aylesbury Pike exit. I planned to take it east along the Miskatonic River until I hit Arkham. But fate, and the Massachusetts state police, had other plans.

They were waiting at the bottom, their patrol cars bisecting the road going both ways. Even in the rain, they stood there in their jack boots and their uniforms, which always looked a little too much like the SS for my taste. I pulled over to the side and got out of my car. There was an officer listening to an animated woman explaining how she had to get back to Ipswich and all the other roads were closed. Something about a dog, though I tried not to listen too closely as I didn't really want to know.

"Ma'am, this road is closed too. All the roads east of here are out. River's flooded. You wouldn't make it more than a few miles. Best to get back onto the interstate and head west."

The officer's voice was even and friendly, but the woman wasn't listening. She just kept telling him the same story, that she had to get to Ipswich.

"You gotta go west, ma'am, that's the only way that's open. West."

Go west. I'd heard it a thousand times, repeated like a mantra. Go west. West to where it was dry, where the rivers hadn't broken their binds and risen to heights from which they would never again retreat. Go west and maybe there'd be some hope there. Go west until they started telling you to go east, 'cause that meant you'd gone too far.

I glanced at the other cars stopped on the side of the road under the beating rain. No one else was approaching the officer. This woman spoke for us all. But soon she was in tears, and the officer didn't know how to handle her. There was just too much suffering going on in the world for him to comfort this one woman. It just wasn't possible. At which point I approached the man who I'd known I'd approach from the moment I arrived, for he was the only one of us who seemed not at all bothered by the rain.

He was standing next to the beat-up pickup truck I'd bought off a guy for the trip, probably on its last legs when I was born. He looked up at me with unblinking eyes, water sliding down his nearly hairless scalp, across a broad forehead, onto the great, flat nose that dominated his face.

"That a four-wheel drive?" he asked as I approached.

"It is."

"We'll need it where we're going."

"We?"

"You're going east, ain't you? I need to get east too, farther than you, I'd suppose. With the staties blocking the main road, we'll have to take the back way. Most of them ain't paved, and with this rain they'll be hard to pass, if we can pass at all."

"You headed to Innsmouth?"

His face reshaped itself into something I guessed was a smile.

"You really have to ask, friend?"

"I try not to judge a book by its cover."

"That's mighty progressive of you, but the look is the look, and ain't no use running from who you are. Didn't used to be this bad," he said, glancing over at the sideview mirror on my truck. "I dare say it wasn't near this bad a week ago. It's strange times, I guess. Lots of things are changing." He looked back at me. "But I've heard the call, and that's all that matters now. I need to get home."

"If you can get me there, I can take you as far as Arkham."

He regarded me with his wet, blue eyes that never blinked, then shook his head.

"No good. Arkham is the wrong direction. East yes, but south. I need to get north."

"It's a straight shot north from Arkham up the federal highway."

He furrowed his brow, and I could see that he was considering his other options, few that they were. As for me, I had none.

"Tell you what. You get me to Arkham, you can have the truck. I'll get myself back out, one way or another."

He squinted his narrow eyes at me. "You sure about that, mister? Why are you so desperate to get to Arkham anyway?"

"I am sure, and my business is my own."

"Fair enough. I'll let you drive till Arkham."

He followed me back to my truck and climbed in the passenger side, filling the cab with the smell of the sea. I glanced back at the troopers, who were still urging the woman to turn around and go back. Little scenes like that were taking place all over the world, some with more violence than others. I pulled back onto the interstate and looked at him.

"So what now?"

"Go back west," he said. "Sometimes to get to a place, you gotta leave it behind."

I sighed. West was more of a parking lot than a road. I rolled down the window. The rain was still pouring, but I needed the air.

"Sorry, friend," the man said. He didn't need to explain further.

"Name's Andrew," I said. "Andrew Beckett."

"Franklin Olmstead," he said.

"You from Innsmouth, I take it?" I had to speak up over the sound of honking horns. Traffic crawled and the rain fell.

He shook his head. "Grew up in Kansas City. Innsmouth wasn't a word that was spoken very openly in my household. I can remember my parents arguing when I was young. They'd get into these violent, absolute drag-out fights. Murder was in the air, but I was too young to know it. That was how I first heard the word. I remembered it because they were yelling at each other at the top of their lungs. But not that word. Even then, they said it only in whispers. That's the kind of thing that stands out, even to a child."

"I've heard things about it, but nothing solid. I never really understood why so many people try to get away."

"Try and fail," he said. "My grandfather left there right before the purges began. He killed himself before I was born. Shot himself with a Colt 45. My father killed himself when I was 12. Same gun." He reached his hand inside his coat and pulled out a pistol. It was a 1911, a fine weapon. He looked at it, and when I saw his eyes I wondered if he'd ever thought about following in his forebearers footsteps. "Anyway. I need to know."

"What exit are we looking for?" I asked. I wasn't trying to change the subject, but I wasn't sure I wanted to continue on this one either.

"The next one," he said. "Only a couple more miles."

A couple more miles that might take hours to pass. I swung the car into a cut in the median, past a sign warning that it was for emergency vehicles only. Then we were running west down the empty eastbound lanes. Even when the world was ending, most people were obeying the traffic rules. Somehow I didn't think the troopers were interested in giving any tickets. In my rearview, I watched as others followed my lead, crossing the median behind me. It was a tiny crack in the façade of the lie that law and order still ruled, one of many that were breaking out across the country. It wouldn't be long before the whole thing would fall.

***

It's hard to say when the sun set that evening. The thick clouds and endless rain blocked the light even when the sun still shone. So it was full dark when we reached the outskirts of Arkham. Along the way were scenes of ruin. Broken-down cars, burned-out houses, flooded fields. We road down backroads in silence. Three times we pulled off the road behind a copse of trees when we saw headlights approaching. Whether the police or final stragglers who could not bring themselves to leave, we didn't know. And we didn't want to find out. Desperation was taking hold, and violence would ride in its wake. Two other times the road was blocked by barricades, but nothing the two of us couldn't handle.

When we climbed out of the truck a second time, the air was different. Thicker. Heavy, with the tang of ammonia.

"It should smell of the sea," Franklin said. He was right. The Miskatonic River flowed through Arkham on its way to the Atlantic. But with Boston underwater and the coast of Massachusetts presumably shifted inland for all time, the ocean could not be that far away. "But the world is changing." I didn't ask him what that meant.

We moved the second barricade out of the way. There was a faded sign just beyond it, leaning to the point that it would probably fall within the year, if it wasn't covered with water by then. *Arkham, it read, 3 miles.*

We walked back to the truck, but Franklin stopped, his hand still on the door handle. In the distance was the sound of thunder.

"We should be careful now," he said. "It's too dangerous to drive any farther. We should walk."

"Walk?"

"Yes. There was a turn-off a quarter mile back. We hide the truck and walk the rest of the way into town."

I glanced down the darkened road ahead. The rain, for the blessed moment, had stopped. But it was still wet and heavy and hot. Hotter than I'd ever known it to be on a night like this in Massachusetts. I did not look forward to the walk.

"If we should walk, then we're here," I said to him. I reached inside and grabbed my bag. I pulled out a 9mm Sig Saur, chambered a round, and slipped it into a holster on my belt. "And if we're here, then you did your bit. I can take it the rest of the way." I reached out my hand to him. "Good luck, Franklin." He looked at it, and then shook his bulbous head.

"I said I'd get you to town. We aren't in town yet. I'll take you in, make sure you get there safe. Then the rest is up to you."

He shouldered past me to stare down the road.

"If you're coming along," I said, "you'll need a weapon. I don't expect we'll see much, but you never know."

Franklin opened his coat to show the 1911 holstered there, and then looked back over his shoulder into the darkness ahead of us.

"I wish I could agree with you."

***

A half mile down the road, it started to rain again. I was glad for it. Up until that point, it had been like walking through a suspended ocean, and my clothes were soaked already. Somehow it was better this way. Franklin gestured to a house that sat back about 20 feet from the road. It was covered in vines and ivy. I'd seen things like that before, in the South, where the kudzu moves like an animal-thing, creeping up and over buildings and swallowing them in its great green embrace. Things move and crawl beneath it, but men do not see, cannot see. It is a world alone and separate, and we'd just assume keep it that way.

But I'd never seen anything like that in Massachusetts. I might have not thought much of it, were this not the sixth or seventh house we'd seen like that. Franklin gestured, but he didn't say anything. It was enough. *The world has changed.* No, that's not quite right. The world *is changing.* That was it. That was the ticket. We were walking into something, but we couldn't have avoided it. Not forever. Whatever this was, it was creeping too. Moving from the sea that had given it birth. Inexorably, until it would be all there was. Somerson hadn't been crazy after all, and that opened up so many possibilities, some more hopeful than others.

We kept moving.

"Innsmouth is probably under water," I said, it suddenly striking me that the seaside town could not have survived the flood.

Franklin had been walking ahead of me. He stopped, and looking over his shoulder he gave me a thin-lipped smile. "The body returns to the sea," he said. "The corpse of a town may well have sunken into the depths. But its heart never left the deep. It was always there, waiting." Then he turned around and kept walking, and I decided to choose silence.

I've seen many things in this life. I've been places that they write about only in the forbidden books, the ones that our wise elders burned in the old days and that our contemporaries bury in library vaults. I've seen enough to know what is possible in the wilds, what secrets the untraveled spaces of our planet hold. Now it felt like those spaces were opening up. I wasn't going to them anymore. They were coming to me.

The rumble in the distance refined itself. As we walked through an inky darkness that I'd seldom experienced in the States, the sound began to resolve itself into something that wasn't thunder. I'd heard the sound before. Many times. It was a motorcycle, the kind for which "muffler" is a dirty word.

"Police?" I said to Franklin as we heard one roar off into some unseen distance. He shook his head, the few wet strands of hair that still sprung from his head slinging water in every direction.

"No. Something else. Stay quiet now. Keep to the shadows."

I pulled my pistol from my belt. He squinted at it.

"No, not yet. You use that and they'll all come."

"Who?"

He shrugged. "Does it matter?"

He was right about that. I looked at the gun for a second and then jammed it back into its holster. We'd play it his way for now.

We kept on, but only a few hundred feet down the road Franklin jerked a thumb toward the forest. We stepped into the canopy of trees and slid behind one of their trunks. I didn't know what had set him off, but I figured it was better not to ask. I heard the roar of an engine again, and realized after a time that it was growing louder. Franklin slipped his pistol out of his coat and looked at me. *Just in case.* The roar was upon us, and the motorcycle came into view.

It was a Harley, as I expected. The guy on it was like out of a movie. Big, bearded, with tattoos down his arms that showed through his leather cuts. He rolled down the street another hundred feet from where we were hiding. He stopped for a second. Looked. Listened. I flattened myself against the tree. He couldn't have seen us, I knew that. But as I watched him, it was almost like he was sniffing the air. But whatever it was passed in a second. He turned the bike around and roared back down the street past us and off into the distance until he went over a hill and disappeared.

I was about to say something to Franklin when the expression on his face stopped me cold. Franklin's skin was like the underbelly of a fish, sickly pale and permanently slick. But if it was possible for someone who looked like that to blanche, he'd just done it. There was fear between the slits of his eyelids too.

"You all right?"

"It's nothing," he said, too quickly. It was the first time he'd lied to me. "Let's just keep moving. Stick to the trees."

It was easier said than done. The constant rain had turned the ground to mud, and ditches were now raging rivers. The going was slow enough that it wasn't long before we abandoned caution and returned to the roads. We'd been walking for about another half mile when we saw light in the distance, cutting through the darkness and chasing us back into the woods. We hid behind a large oak and stared down the road, but this light never moved. Whatever it was, it was stationary. We crept forward through the muck, this time not daring the open road. I'm not sure what I thought we would find, but what we did was somehow worse than whatever I was imagining.

It was a car, one of those old deals that drove like a boat and took up three quarters of the road. The lights were on, shining into the night from the driveway of a house. The driver's side door was open, as was the trunk. Franklin stared at it for so long it made me uncomfortable.

"What are you thinking?"

"I'm thinking we can't leave it behind us without checking it out," he said. "Could be some sort of a trap."

"If it's a trap, then won't we be walking into it?"

"Maybe," he said. "But I prefer to face whatever I'm up against head on than to have it crawling up my back."

"Fair enough," I said, and I pulled my pistol for at least the fourth time already. I'd thought this job would be tough. Even dangerous. But the unknown was so much worse than a straight-up fight.

We stood there for a minute, just listening. It was silent, save for the steady fall of rain. But I'd been listening to that for so long I barely heard it anymore. It was like the sound of my own breathing, or of the heart beating in my chest. Above that and beyond that was nothing. No sound of roaring engines. And no sound of life in the house we were looking at.

There was nothing special about the building itself. Two stories, with the high slanted roofs people in New England prefer so that the snow slides right off instead of accumulating. It was rain that rolled off it now. The front door was open. That, combined with the state of the car, told you that whoever had lived here had been well into the process of moving out when whatever happened...happened.

Franklin held his gun low and to his side, like somebody who knew how to use it. We crept up the drive, and I felt terribly exposed. Franklin swung around the driver's side door and leveled his pistol. I came up behind him, but saw nothing.

"Car's on," Franklin said, "but out of gas." He reached his hand toward the switch for the car's lights, but thought better of it. "God," he said, a fish-belly white hand covering his nose, "that smell."

For it to bother him, it must have been bad. Then the wind shifted and I smelled it too. So overwhelming as to almost knock you over. Ammonia so thick I felt like I was standing in the middle of a factory making cleaning products.

"Clean freaks, maybe," I offered lamely.

"Right."

He looked from the car to the front door.

"They'd left the car on while they moved out. Wanted to be able to go in a hurry." He walked around to the open trunk and looked inside. Suitcases, now soaked. "Something interrupted them."

I glanced down the roadway in the direction of town. "Guys on the motorcycles, maybe?"

"Maybe. Let's check out the house."

I was not a fan of this proposal, but he didn't ask me before he started toward the open door. As we approached, the stench of ammonia was so thick, if you'd told me they'd bathed the house in it, I'd have believed you. We crept inside as I wondered why I hadn't thought to bring a flashlight. The shadows were pervasive, and even when my eyes adjusted I could see little. But what I did see was peculiar.

The house was entirely ordinary, exactly what you'd expect to see if someone was moving out in a hurry. Chaos, yes, but ordered chaos. No signs of a struggle. No signs that they'd been interrupted. It was just as if they'd been in the middle of moving and then stopped. Just walked out the front door and left the car behind and the door open.

We moved into the hallway. The pictures told us this was a stereotypical family. Mom and dad, two children, boy and girl. The boy played baseball. The girl was too young for such things yet. The bedrooms told the same story as the living room. Clothes lay on the beds, neatly waiting to be packed away. Nothing was ransacked. Nothing, that I could see, was stolen.

As I stepped out of what had been the girl's room, my foot landed on a crumped piece of clothing in the hallway. I kicked it with my shoe. It was a t-shirt. There was a rainbow emblazoned across the top of it, with a unicorn beneath it. *I believe*, it said on the bottom. I reached down to pick it up, but my hand stopped short.

I wouldn't have thought it possible to grow accustomed to the smell of ammonia, but during our time in the house my nose had adjusted. But as I reached for the shirt, it came back with a vengeance, like the tiny piece of child's clothing was soaked in it.

I felt it before I heard anything. A pressure, a change in the air. A fresh blast of that acrid smell. Then a sound above us as the trees bent in the wind. I started to speak, but Franklin held up a fleshy hand.

I stopped, and my breath stopped too. If it hadn't, I might have screamed at what came next. There was a massive thud above us, like one of those trees outside had broken free from the earth and smashed down on the roof. The entire house shook, and a chunk of ceiling plaster fell to the floor beside me.

The pistol in my hand shook as another thud landed on the roof. If you'd told me that in that moment some ancient giant strode across the top of the house, I'd have believed you. But it wasn't footsteps I heard, even massive ones. It was more like the movement of an enormous mass lumbering across the tiles. There was another thud, and then the trees groaned and creaked again as they swung back and forth.

We didn't speak for a minute in the silence that followed. I'm not sure I even breathed.

"It's gone."

I looked at Franklin, who suddenly seemed far more knowledgeable about all this than he should have. "And what the fuck was *it*?"

"The world is changed, remember," he said. Then he turned and walked out of the bedroom, down the hall, and back out the front door.

I followed, angry. "If you know what's going on, you need to let me know."

"I didn't make you come here."

"That's not really the point now, is it? We're in this together until we both get what we came for. You know something. Or you suspect it at least."

He sighed and stared down at me. "Pay attention," he said. "What do you notice?"

I looked around. I didn't notice much of anything. Then I did, at least a few things. The smell, for one. I won't say it was gone, but it had lessened considerably. And the wind. There was none. And despite the constant rain, I realized there hadn't been any the whole time we'd been outside.

"But something bent the trees," he said, reading my mind.

"Something?"

"There's stories my grandmother used to tell me," he said as I followed him back to the road. "About creatures that were not what they were born to be, but were made into something else. Twisted and formed to do the bidding of their masters."

I didn't know what stories his grandmother might tell, but I'd read of such things in forbidden books in dark tombs and library dungeons. *Shoggoths*, I whispered so quietly no one could have heard me, but Franklin smiled nonetheless.

"That's what they were called, yes. This is something different, I think. But all the same too."

***

We avoided the forest, and not for the rain. Whatever had moved through the trees was out there, and maybe more like it. We'd take our chances with the bikers. But they never came, and we made our way down the empty road past a sign that read, *Welcome to Arkham.*

"You ever been to Arkham before?" Franklin said.

"No."

"This road ahead, it leads directly into town. Right through the middle of it. Heads over the river and dead-ends at the gates of Miskatonic. It's the best way in and out. I'd say we were home free. But they'll be waiting."

"Who exactly do you think they are?"

Franklin shrugged, but even in the movement there was a lie. "Probably came through, saw an opportunity to steal shit after the city emptied. I don't know. I don't know that much about motorcycle gangs."

Coincidentally, I did. Back during a brief stint as a reporter, when I'd thought I could satiate my need for adventure in a respectable profession. I was wrong, both about the profession and about my needs. But I'd learned a little about a lot of things. I'd spent some time as a runner for the Hell's Angels. They were criminals, sure. Liked to run drugs and girls and occasionally killed people when it was necessary. But they'd never taken over an entire town before. That was basically unthinkable. That was Hollywood trash. So what exactly was this all about?

I considered things were just different now, that maybe this was the future, like something out of the old *Dawn of the Dead* movie. But that felt wrong too. I could feel it, and I knew Franklin could too. But Franklin wasn't talking. Whatever we'd seen back there, or thought we'd seen, had spooked him. The end of the world had not seemed to faze him. But the bikers—and whatever was moving through those trees—that got to him. I couldn't blame him for the second. I felt the same way. But the other intrigued me.

So I did the only thing I knew to do. I changed the subject. If I could get him talking, maybe something would shake loose.

"What are you going to do, once you get to Innsmouth?" I asked, as for the first time the wind picked up and shook the trees, unleashing a downpour as great as any from the heavens. I was soaked though. I'd forgotten what it meant to be dry and wondered if I'd ever remember.

Franklin shrugged his already slouching shoulders.

"That's not really the point," he said. "I think I'll know when I get there. I had to make a decision, a long time ago, whether I'd follow my father and my grandfather, or if I would take a different path," he said. His eyes never left the road ahead of him. "I don't suppose many people can really understand what that's like, or what it means. But I had the true Marsh blood. That's what my grandma told me, right after my father killed himself. And when she said it..." He just shook his head. "Anyway, I felt pretty normal until I was about thirteen. That's when the change started. Most kids grow facial hair and start liking girls. I felt the call of the sea. But if I'm being honest with you..." He stopped walking and pulled out that 1911. "When I said earlier I thought about eating a bullet, just like my daddy did, I'd decided to do that until whatever it is that happened happened. And then, my friend, it wasn't just a call I heard. It was like something reached inside my chest and pulled me here. So I'll go to Innsmouth. And I'll find what I find. And I'll know what to do. Now let's keep walking. Something is watching us."

I felt the blood drain from my face. I spun around, stared wide-eyed into the forest. Franklin grabbed my arm and jerked me around, pulling me down the road.

"Don't look," he growled. "Whatever it is, we don't want it to think we saw it. Just keep moving."

We moved along the roadway, and in the distance, we heard the roar of another motorcycle, but not one coming in our direction.

"Did you see his jacket?" Franklin asked, as the roar died away.

I had, but I hadn't noticed anything special about it, so I just shook my head.

Franklin gulped down air. "You know about the purge, right? The liquidation?"

"It's not exactly something they teach in grade school in Massachusetts, but yeah, I've heard of it. When the government moved on Innsmouth in the 20s, right? Rounded everybody up and shipped them to concentration camps?"

He nodded his head. "Yeah, 1927. They didn't destroy the town or anything. Just tried to empty it out. They couldn't hold everybody forever, even back then. But there were always stories about what happened to the folks in the camps. Medical experiments, things like that. I never put much stock into tall tales, but maybe I shoulda. But when they let everybody go, they did it with a warning. We had to reform. Change our ways. And most important, we had to ban the Order."

I'd heard of the Order of Dagon, of course. Growing up in Massachusetts, you couldn't miss it. We told stories about it around campfires, scared each other by claiming that the Order would meet in clearings in the forests behind our houses. It wasn't till I was older that I found out the Order had actually existed, that it was a real and solid thing.

"Must have been hard, getting rid of something that had been a part of the town's culture for so long."

I doubted Franklin's slack face was capable of showing much in the way of emotion, but I could have sworn he grinned. "It would have been, so they didn't. It went underground, changed and morphed into different things. The jacket that guy was wearing? It said *Sons of Dagon* on it. The cult didn't die. It evolved. You never know where you might find them."

"And now they've come to Arkham?"

"And now they've come to Arkham."

"But why?"

"If I had to guess? The same reason you've come."

We walked on through the night. It should have been full dark by then, but it wasn't. The thick clouds glowed an unnatural yellow-green. The light made everything look sickly, and it cast a pall on Franklin's face that made him hard to stomach. I kept my eyes on the road instead, until he put a hand on my chest and stopped me.

He nodded toward a service road that intersected with the main drag. It was narrow and choked with thick trees that loomed over both sides of the pavement so far that they seemed to converge in the middle to form a tunnel of vegetation.

"We've been lucky to come this far and not get found out," he said. Not too far away—uncomfortably close, to be honest—a motorcycle engine roared as if to punctuate his statement. "If we take this road, there's another way into town. What do you think?"

The engine roared again, closer. I nodded, and Franklin didn't wait before he struck off onto the broken pavement. If this road was used by anyone, it wasn't used often. The trees blocked out even the sickly glow of the sky, and it was dark underneath them. I remembered that something had been following us from the forest for some time, and I wondered if it would simply step into the clearing and show itself. More than once my heart stopped at a rustling beside us, but whatever it was remained in shadow. Then the road started to open up as the trees fell away.

It was full night, but I wondered if it would ever be dark again. The terrain is varied in that part of New England. Not the flat plains you might find in the great west, or the old mountains to the north, worn down with age. It's a land of piled stone and moss-covered boulders larger than a man, some of which to the untrained eye look like they were placed there by giant hands in times long gone by. That was Arkham too, and the little road passed among those great stones and over little hills, until we came to a rise with a circle of darkness cut into the middle of it. It was a train tunnel.

"The old A&I ran through here, the Anchorhead and Innsmouth line. Last train probably passed through half a century ago, but the tunnel remains. Innsmouth folk would go this way when they didn't want to travel the main road. My people have learned to walk in the shadows."

We stood there, staring into the gaping maw of the tunnel, the sound of the trees bending in the wind surrounding us. This was it, I guessed. There was no light inside. No way to see what was in front of your face. Franklin sort of shrugged his drooping shoulders and moved forward. I followed, but at last I remembered my phone. I'd kept it with me, those past few days, even though it had been useless since the event. But suddenly I realized I didn't need a flashlight. I already had one.

As we stepped from the gloom of night into the total darkness of the tunnel, I turned it on. To say I was disappointed in the effect is an understatement. The light barely penetrated the darkness. It was so complete, so *thick*.

The tunnel could not have been more than a few hundred yards long, but it seemed as though it stretched away for miles. I could see the dim light at the end of the tunnel, but it didn't give me the comfort the old saw would make you think it would. Franklin pushed forward, stepping steadily but carefully. My feet splashed into cold puddles and I stumbled across obstacles I could not see and did not care to guess at.

I was taken back to my childhood, standing at the top of the stairs that led down into my parents' basement. They might as well have descended into the abyss, such was the darkness of that ancient root cellar. I was afraid then, and I was afraid now.

But Franklin didn't stop. He moved with such swiftness, such sureness, that I wondered if his altered eyes saw farther into the night than I could. I tramped after him, following the sound of his footsteps.

The footsteps stopped. I opened my mouth to ask why and almost retched, the stench of ammonia fell upon me with such completeness.

"Run."

I hesitated.

"Run!"

My mind was in a blur. I rushed into the darkness, racing toward the circle of light bobbing up and down with every stretch. Franklin screamed somewhere behind me, a low-pitched guttural shriek unlike anything I'd ever heard. It was made all the worse by the simple fact that whatever attacked him made no sound at all. Just the smell. The smell of ammonia.

It filled my nostrils and stung my throat. I coughed as I ran and my lungs burned like fire, but I did not dare to stop. With every footfall, it grew thicker, stronger, more rank. And then I felt it.

I knew what the feeling was, intellectually speaking. I'd heard of it before, the landscape of fear. It's something prey feel when a predator is in their midst. A preternatural feeling deep in their bones, down to the pit of their soul, a sensation older than smell or taste. I felt it now. I was surrounded by something inexplicable. Deadly.

I closed my eyes, waiting for my doom to befall me, and I gave it one last push, one last dash, stumbling down to my knees as I went. I felt the hand of death close in around me. But then it withdrew as quickly as it came, and I felt the cold rush of fresh air around me. I'd made it.

I opened my eyes.

A shotgun was six inches from my face.

"Well, well, well," a bearded man in a ragged leather jacket said, chuckling. "What do we have here?" There was a rush of movement, followed by a sharp pain, and the world faded into darkness.

***

I awoke to the crackling of a fire and the smell of smoke. I was inside, but I saw nothing save for the shadows that danced upon the ceiling from the light of the hearth.

"The end of the world makes you appreciate the little things," came the deep timbre of a man's voice. "Like a fire in this unending rain."

I followed the voice to a great oaken desk that sat in front of huge windows that ran from the floor to the ceiling. A man sat there, smoking a cigar, leaned back in his chair with his legs propped up like there was nowhere else he should ever be. His black boots rested on the desk, matching the leather jacket he was wearing. He smiled behind a gray beard that came to a point below his chin in a way that reminded me of the devil.

I sat up on the leather couch. I wasn't bound or restrained in any way. The man swung his legs off the desk and reached for a decanter of brown liquid. He poured a generous glass and got up. He walked around to where I sat and handed it to me.

"Sorry about your head. This will help."

As if he willed it into existence, suddenly a sharp pain threatened to split my skull in two. I took the glass, and he stood, staring down at me. He didn't move till I downed it.

"Let me know if you want some more," he said, before he turned and walked back to the desk. He was wearing the same jacket I'd seen on the road, with *Sons of Dagon* written across the back. But it was what was printed beneath it that haunted me, that image from which I could not pull my gaze. It was a visage I'd only seen in the darkest tomes in the blackest temples that I'd had the misfortune to visit. The image was never quite the same. Sometimes the tentacles were in greater number, sometimes they were longer or shorter. But the eyes. Those eyes beneath a brow of hate, that was always the same.

"I have to say, Mr. Beckett, I'm very familiar with your work. I didn't expect to see you here, but it's auspicious, nevertheless. You can call me Goat."

I suppressed my surprise. Whoever this man was, there was nothing about him that would lead one to believe he was all that active in the antiquities trade. "Well," I said, "I guess I wanted to see Miskatonic before it became a ruin. I've heard so much about it."

The man leaned against the desk and smiled. "A tourist then? How quaint. But you're right. It wouldn't surprise me if most of the coast is beneath the sea soon, my beloved alma mater included."

"You attended Miskatonic?" I asked in surprise before I could stop myself.

"Oh, this," he said, pointing to his jacket. "We all wear disguises, Mr. Beckett. We all wear masks. You'd be surprised. This country is more tolerant of a biker gang than it is of a faith it does not understand. So we adapt. What masks do you wear, Mr. Beckett? You are a thief, and I do not use that word as an insult," he added, no doubt seeing the look cross my face. "A thief in the line of the great Satampra Zeiros. My grandfather would read me stories of him when I was a child. You are his heir. And that's why you are here, isn't it? Oh, the architecture is grand," he said, sweeping the room with his hand. "They built this office for the librarian, god's sake. Though old man Armitage certainly earned it. But yes, you didn't come to here to admire the tapestries, did you?"

"No," I said, not caring for deception, "I did not. And I'd like to leave here in one piece if it's all the same to you."

"That is entirely up to you. I have no interest in killing you, Mr. Beckett. And frankly," he turned and looked out the high windows to where the rain continued to pour, "I doubt you are likely to survive anyway. None of us are. So what do you say?"

"You haven't told me what you want, but I guess I don't have much choice but to agree."

He grinned. "Good man. But if I had to bet, I'd say I want the same thing that brought you here. I want you to retrieve the book."

The air grew chill as he said the words, even though he did not say the book's name. It was close enough to hear and to know.

"I'm not going to ask how you guessed."

"A man like you would be here for no other reason. It's what brought us here too."

"Then why do you need me?"

He barked out a little laugh. "You don't think it's that easy, do you? The man who once held this office did everything in his power to make sure that book never fell into the...should I say the wrong hands or the right ones?"

"I guess it depends on your perspective."

"So it does. Let us just say unauthorized hands."

"I suppose you'll want me to deal with the security precautions, and I dare say they will be the kind that the university's insurance carrier wouldn't cover."

"Ha! No, my friend. If it were only that, we wouldn't need you. I have men who can hack a computer, crack a safe. Take a bullet for me, if need be."

"But that's not the biggest problem, is it?"

Goat pulled the top off the decanter and smirked. He poured himself a taller glass than mine and raised it to me in salute. "You've done your homework."

"You don't think this is the first time I've been asked to...acquire the book, do you? No, I know all about its special charms. I'm just finally desperate enough to go for it."

"Then you know that the book calls the one it belongs to. You do not acquire it. It acquires you. And anyone who presumes to claim the book without first being asked will pay for their arrogance."

"And I take it the book has not called to you?"

The smirk faded and I saw the man's careful control fall away if only for a second. His face reddened ever so slightly, and he swallowed hard.

"I've read the stories. I know how this works. There's a reason you won't take the book. You know what happens to people who try to possess it when it's not theirs to possess. Why would I take that chance?"

"It's the only chance you have. We've been in this game a long time. I think we know how it ends."

"So I get the book, give it to you, and you just let me go?"

"You get the book and you give it to me and I'll let you go. There are things worse than us...out there."

"What are you going to do with it?"

"There's a new order coming, Mr. Beckett. My people have had a bootheel on them for too long. We've done our service to the Old Ones. It's time for our reward."

"If you've done your service, why do you need the book?"

"Well, I don't trust many men. Why should I trust the gods who created them?"

"Seems like a dangerous game to play."

"I'll worry about that. You worry about the book."

The door opened and two men entered, each armed with a mean-looking shotgun. My friend Franklin wasn't the only one with the "Innsmouth Look." Whether Goat was lying to me or not, I couldn't know. But that these two men were from that cursed town, I could not doubt. The world had fallen into insanity. A bastard faith, hunted to extinction, a cult transformed into little more than a criminal gang. But I'd dealt with gangs before. I understood them, how they worked. I didn't understand the rest, but I figured I didn't need to either.

"You got a deal. I'll get your book."

"Excellent," he said, rising. "Follow me. We don't have far to go."

We walked out into the great vaulted floor of the library, down the spiraling steel staircase outside his second-story office to the marble floor below. The library was ancient by American standards, having stood there now for 500 years. It was, in many ways, as legendary as the tomes it was said to hold. Constructed, according to legend, in a single night by a group of men who came hooded and cloaked aboard black ships under cover of darkness, in the midst of a raging storm. Only to leave, under the same circumstances, but not before constructing the edifice that one day would become the library. There were some who said it looked more like a temple, and others more like a tomb. For my part, I'd not mind seeing it burned to the ground, with no two stones remaining on top of each other.

I had never been to Miskatonic, but I'd studied the layout of the library before. Past clients had inquired about securing certain artifacts from within it. I'd never taken them up on the offer. The security was said to be state of the art, the vault impenetrable. Laser tripwires and timing mechanism-activated seals. And then there were the more esoteric protections that some claimed were in place. Whatever was true, if Goat was wrong and his people couldn't handle the traps, it would be a short trip. I'm not sure how I ever intended to get the book. I just figured things would work out. They tended to. And now Goat was both my potential doom and my salvation.

We walked through another set of double doors into a dark room, lit only by our flashlights.

"We've been working here for a couple days." I saw ripped-out cables littered across the floor and cracked security screens plugged into computers running on battery packs. "It took us a while to break the first few seals."

"And now you want me to rip open the seventh one?"

Goat chuckled. "Something like that."

We passed through the open vault door into another chamber, this one I was surprised to see still with lighting.

"Every light on the East Coast is off," Goat said. "But the generator still works in this one. Shows you their priorities."

I stood there and stared. In a case in a recessed niche in the wall, as if there for worship, sat the crimson-bound book, its golden lettering shimmering in the pale light. I could read it, read it as if it had been written in English 40,000 years ago, or whenever alien hands had first inked it.

There are books that are said to be magical. In fact, of those there are an abundance, the great fires of the Inquisition having barely made a dent in their number. But although some may claim they are magical, the truth of that statement is difficult to prove with most. But not with the *Incendium Maleficarum*, for it had magic written across its cover. Any man or woman, regardless of their race or language, could read the name of the *Inferno of the Witch*.

Goat held out a hand. From his fist fell a leather cord. A key hung upon it.

"As I said, of the many measures taken by the university to protect it, only one remains. And that is the one that only the book bears. You must take it."

"And if I do, what difference will that make? Even if I give it to you, that won't make it yours."

"We've studied this question, the metaphysics of it. And we've determined that the book, if given freely to another, protects the one who would receive it from its power."

"But let me guess," I said. "The metaphysics don't say the same for the one who gives it."

Goat shook his head, with a look one might mistake for genuine regret.

"I'm afraid that is accurate."

I reached out my hand and took the leather cord, felt the silver key in my palm.

"Well, seeing as I don't have much choice..."

"Seeing as you don't," Goat said, handing it to me.

I walked around a case in the center of the room and glanced down but for a moment. That's all I needed to take my breath away. Inside lay the *Necronomicon*, a tome as shrouded in ancient myth and mystery as the one I'd come to take.

"I already have a copy of *that*," Goat said, noticing my interest. "You can take it with you on the way out, if you please. You might need it."

I tore my eyes away from a prize that at one time I would have killed men to have, and continued my lonely walk to almost certain death. To where the book lay, waiting. I held the key in my hand. I slid it into the lock. And then, I heard something that grabbed hold of my mind and would not let go.

It started as a small, sharp sound, like that of a crystal goblet shattering. Then a throbbing, a drumming. Not in my ears, but in my chest. Then the piping, piping that seemed without rather than within, as if it flowed upon noxious winds from some great distance. I found myself looking around the room for the source of the demonic sound. Goat stood staring at me, without a hint of recognition or even curiosity on his face. I was afraid, he figured, and delaying the inevitable. But it wasn't that. It wasn't that at all.

There are legends older than man, come down to us through the ages, written in books almost as forbidden as the one that now sat before me, that speak of the ways of things. Goat was right. The book chooses its master, and it would punish those who sought to take it without permission for their insolence. But how does one know? How does one know if the book has chosen you? As with all things, there are signs. And the greatest of those was the song, the song that calls to the man who would be its master.

In that instant, it sang for me.

I turned, looked down at the floor. I had but a few moments to think, to decide what I should do. I stared at the cracked stone, struggling to piece together a way out of that room. The two guards clutched their shotguns. If I went for one, the other would take me down. I was certain that Goat had a weapon as well, and I did not wish to fight him. I won't say that I've never killed a man, but I knew that Goat has killed more and was better at it. As I stared at those cracks, thinking, wishing that they would just break free from beneath me, I realized something. The cracks were awfully uniform. They weren't so much cracks as straight lines, and those rarely happen in nature. I looked back up at the book and I realized the truth. Goat had been wrong. There was one more security measure, one so dramatic that I chuckled audibly at it.

"Only in Miskatonic," I whispered under my breath.

I turned the lock and heard it pop open. I lifted the glass. The book sat on its pillow. I turned and looked at Goat.

"The book," I said.

"Bring it to me."

I glanced back at it. "You know, I think I'll keep it."

I grabbed the book and lifted it from its resting place. I heard the pressure mechanism, the one I knew was beneath that pillow, pop as the weight that held it down was released. And then, so fast that I didn't even have time to think about it, the floor dropped out from underneath me.

I hit the ground below with a thud, rolling to my side and hoping that nothing shattered. A shotgun blast peppered the ground where I'd lain only a second before. I heard shouted commands from above. I didn't have much time to think. They'd be after me in an instant. The room was pitch black, and I thanked Goat for the flashlight he'd given me as we made our way through the darkened library. There would be a door, I knew, but it would also be locked. This was, after all, a trap. My reprieve might be a brief one. But I also knew that whoever built this trap would not have been the person who built the library. This more modern accommodation would not be without a weakness. The sound of rushing water told me I was right.

A stream flowed through the cavern where I stood. My flashlight revealed a river coursing from a breach in the stone wall. I followed that flow to the other wall, and said a prayer to whatever gods were above, thanking them, for the passage through the far wall looked just large enough to accommodate a man.

All of this happened in but an instant. I had no time to think, no time to calculate. I grabbed the book, and as I heard one of Goat's men land with a grunt on the ground beside me, I threw myself into the water. I was grabbed instantly, slammed against the wall as I was pulled by the current through the opening. I gasped, swallowing water, and struggled for the surface. My flashlight was lost, and I clung to the book as if it were more important than life itself. There was nothing to do but give in to the pull of a current coursing through a chasm that might well head to the center of the earth for all I knew.

With some effort, I flipped on my back, and now for the first time I had some control. The cavern widened, and the water flowed quickly, but maybe not as quickly as before. I floated down this Stygian river, wondering if at any minute it would drop beneath me, taking me to my death. But the river continued to widen, and the flow continued to slow. I realized then that I could see. This should not have been possible. But when I looked down at the book, I knew how, for it glowed with some internal fire. Not enough that one would notice it in the bright light of day. But in a place like this, one so dark that the book must have felt at home? It blazed.

For the second time that night, I heard a noise that immediately changed my perspective on things. This time, not for the better. It was a roar that grew more ferocious with each second, the kind of roar made by water striking solid stone after a fall of hundreds of feet. But even as I thought this would be my death, a rocky shore emerged to my left. I grabbed at it, slipping, before my fingers found purchase. I pulled myself up onto this soaking shore and spat out fetid water. I looked over to my right and realized just how close I had come to death. The black water poured over a ledge not five feet from me. I crept forward and peered over it. I saw nothing but an infinite, thundering abyss.

As I looked down into it, I wondered if my choices were death by slow starvation or a quick plunge into bottomless night. The ledge on which I sat was somewhat dry, but water still flowed around me, over the small ledge and into the greater flow. I realized this could be my salvation. The water had to be coming from somewhere.

By the glow of the book I searched, eyes straining for an opening. And then I saw it, an area of black on black, a darkness a little bit deeper than the rest. It was a passage, a doorway, and water flowed down from somewhere above and out of it. This was my exit. But as I stepped through flowing water to its entrance, something else floated down from above, riding on that flow—the stench of ammonia. I chilled, and the book seemed to flame brighter in confirmation.

In my time in the great northern wastes, I had heard stories of men found dead from starvation in their cabins. Perhaps not an entirely unusual thing, were it not for the stores of food waiting only a few feet from their front doors. I had wondered what kind of fear could make a man embrace certain death, making him fear what was behind his door more than what waited for him if he never opened it. As I stood on the threshold of that tunnel, water rushing around my feet, I knew.

I gripped the book tightly, hoping that it might provide some sort of protection, and took my first step. The hint of ammonia grew with every subsequent footfall until it was so thick that I coughed and gagged, pulling my soaking shirt over my nose to breathe.

The tunnel sloped upward. It was narrow but tall, wide enough for a man to walk without stooping. I tried to tread silently, stealthily, but the splashing of the water echoed like a shout throughout that tunnel. If something was hunting me, it knew precisely where I was.

I'm not sure how long I moved up that path, wondering what watched me, feeling its cold hands on my neck. But at last there came a darkness somehow thicker than before. My heart sank. I'd reached a wall, a dead end.

I ran my hand along the rock, and as I did, water ran over my fingers. There was a wall there, but it wasn't solid. At the bottom, water flowed with some speed, washing around my legs. I knelt down, water up to my chin, and felt blindly at the bottom of the wall. There was a space there, maybe a couple feet in height, where the water had forced its way through. The water was coming from somewhere, and I didn't have a choice but to find out from where. I took a deep breath, and dove beneath the water.

I kicked my feet as hard as I could, but the flow of the water pushed back against me. I kicked again and moved forward, with disturbing sluggishness. The thought of drowning there, inhaling the stinking black water, flashed into my mind. It covered me, and panic began. I might have given in to it had my hand not broken through the water into the air above. I followed it and burst through into life and hope again. I inhaled a breath of ammonia so strong I gagged.

Something brushed against my leg. I spun around, my eyes peering into a room somewhat brighter than the one I'd left. It was a tunnel, and the light came from the end of it. I didn't know if this was a sewer or what had once been a road, but I didn't stop to think or wonder. I splashed over to the side and pulled myself up onto a stone ledge. In the distance, there was a crash of water, as if something impossibly large had emerged from the depths to look and then plunged back beneath. I didn't stop to figure out what it was. I ran, my feet beating splashing tattoos with every footfall.

I emerged into the night, and the rain pounded down upon me. It had been raining before, but this was something entirely different. A hurricane and a nor'easter and a monsoon all wrapped up into one. Lightning flashed and thunder followed. This part of the city was not yet flooded, but water rushed into the tunnel behind me, and I knew that everything I saw would be under the sea by morning. I heard a great splash from the depths of the tunnel, and I ran again. Whatever was ahead was better than what was behind. But such was my fear that I had no plan, no destination, no real thought of escape. I simply ran aimlessly through the streets, stopping only when the roar of a motorcycle drowned out the thunder.

I ducked into the cover of a doorway, cursing myself for running from shadows into the arms of a very real threat. I heard shouting and the roar of more motorcycles moving away from me. I scanned the area from the temporary safety of my doorway. A flash of lightning revealed the spires of Miskatonic in the distance. The underground river had carried me deep into the city center, the business district. Good, in that no one would really look for me there, at least not yet. Bad, in that I was as far from escaping the city as I could possibly be.

I didn't dare tarry for long. Above me, I heard a creaking sound. I looked up as a dark form passed from roof to roof. When that blast of ammonia hit me, I forgot the dangers ahead and ran once again. Through the city, legs pumping, heeding nothing but the overwhelming need to escape. It was visceral, instinctive, born of that reptilian part of the brain passed down from when our ancestors were hunted, from when they were far from the top of the food chain. I darted down side streets, sped down alleys, chased by a shadow I could not comprehend.

The only way out I knew was Main Street, which led to the highway where Franklin and I had branched off into the tunnel. Make it there, and I could escape, but the Miskatonic River lay between me and that main thoroughfare. I knew it would be flooded, but if the bridges were out too...

Above me the dark clouds gathered, the way lit by the rapid-fire crackle of lightning. One blast would burst forth before the rolling thunder of the last had even faded away. The smell, the rain, the thundering, the sound, the fear, all of it coalesced into something like madness. I did not stop to think, but burst out of a side street without even bothering to look at what might be waiting for me. And it was waiting.

I stumbled to a stop at the foot of the Armitage Bridge. The waters of the Miskatonic roared beneath it. In another day, maybe two, that same water would wash the bridge from its foundations. But for now it stood, sturdy and strong. Of that I could not doubt, for well did it hold the weight of Goat and three of his brothers. Goat sat on his motorcycle, leaned forward, one arm resting on his cocked knee, like he never had any doubt I'd come this way. He held a shotgun in his other hand, and he grinned at me.

"So we meet again. And no harm done, I see." His eyes greedily took in the image of the glowing book I held. "Why don't you just hand that over and we'll be done here. Then you can go on your way, and we'll act like none of this ever happened. You've played the hero well enough. Time to give in to reason."

The other three men each shuffled forward, clutching shotguns identical to the one Goat rested over his knee.

"I don't think so," I said, regaining my defiance if not my composure.

Goat scoffed. "Look around you, man. Don't you see? You're not getting out of here. Neither are the rest of us without that book. It's wasted on you. You don't know how to use it. You don't know the power it has to stop these things. No one does but me. Hand it over, and I'll save the world for you."

Goat didn't look like a man who put too much stock in salvation.

"Or don't give it to me and I'll kill you where you stand."

I glanced over my shoulder, but behind me the alleys had filled with more of the brotherhood. There really was nowhere to go, nowhere but the Miskatonic. I had taken that chance before, but the roaring of the waters told me that this time, that, too, would be a death sentence.

I looked down at the book. I wondered if maybe I should dive into the Miskatonic, let the water carry me and the book away. At least then Goat wouldn't have it. Maybe that was my part to play in all this. Maybe that was the true meaning of my life. The line has to end somewhere, after all. Better to have it end with an act that might atone for everything I'd done before. A sacrifice. At the thought, the song flared in my mind. But I was committed. This is where it would end for me. And then came that smell.

I'll never know precisely what it was, or why it seemed to float in their wake. It was as much a part of their being as the unquenchable fire that blazed in their otherwise dark, soulless eyes. But like any sign, it was their herald, a sign of their coming.

Goat smelled it too. He blanched, and I saw fear in his eyes. I wondered what it took to make a man like that afraid. In but a moment, I found out.

In a flash crash of lightning, a bolt seemed to strike down from the sky into the Miskatonic River itself. Then the roiling water rose like columns of stone, bursting forth so high that the river seemed as though it would become part of the sky itself. But as the water fell away and back down into the flow below, the columns remained. *They* remained.

They stood there, things never meant to walk on land or breathe the air. Their great arms thrust into the sky, tentacles waving like steel cables before their empty, pitiless eyes. I felt the shadow on me and looked up. They loomed above us too, clamoring across the tops of the buildings, hanging from them as if they were meant to rule the skies just as they had always ruled the deepest oceans.

One of Goat's men, the fool, raised his shotgun and fired it point blank into one of the things that stood beside the bridge. If the blast hurt it, it showed no pain, no fear. Instead, the thing lashed out with a tentacle faster than a whipcrack. And in that instant, the man was ripped in half, the scream having not died from his throat before the top half of his body separated cleanly from the bottom. Another man screamed and ran. He'd not made it off the bridge before another thrust fell down upon him, smashing him to the earth, crushing him into marbled jelly.

I didn't move. Not that I was brave or stupid or a fool. Just that in that moment I could not have moved if God Himself had ordered it.

Nothing moved. The creatures loomed over us, towering like ancient sentinels of stone. But they'd shown their strength and they'd shown their speed. The only thing they hadn't shown is what they were waiting for. Then it came, a moment I'll never be able to explain in the little time that is left for me on this earth. The rain ceased, as if some giant spigot had been closed. The thunder stilled; the lightning did not crash. The sky glowed purple with a violet fire from another world. And then that perfect stillness, that absolute silence, was broken by the sound of footsteps. Sodden, soaking footsteps.

A being approached. I do not call it a man, for I knew for certain that whatever it was, it was not that. It was cloaked and hooded, coming from across the river, shambling up to the Armitage Bridge. Goat started at it, this robed thing. Scaled, webbed hands reached up and pulled back the hood that covered its monstrous face.

To say I recognized the thing would not be entirely accurate. I'd never seen anything like it before, nor do I wish to see anything like it ever again. But in its eyes, there was recognition. For the eyes were those of a friend.

"I made a promise to you," it rasped, "for safe passage, in and out. Take what you've come for and go."

Goat began to speak, but the creature silenced him with a single glance. "You have seen what they can do," it said, turning back to me. "Do as I say, or face the judgment."

I held the book close to my chest, made a few halting steps up the Armitage Bridge. But even when he was in striking distance, Goat made no movement to stop me. The meaning of the look in his eyes, however, was clear. This would not be the last time I'd see him.

When I reached the creature that had been Franklin, I stopped and looked at him. I held my breath and did not gag, despite the overwhelming stench of ammonia.

"The 'Innsmouth Look,' huh?"

His face wavered in what I interpreted to be a smile. "You cannot run from who you are. You'd do well to remember that."

"Thank you. For everything."

He nodded and raised the hood back over his head. I turned and took another step, only for him to stop me once again.

"Mr. Beckett. The promise is kept. The debt is paid, and you will have safe passage this night. But when the sun rises, then it falls to them. What is coming, and is to be, none of us can change."

Now I nodded. There was nothing left to say and no point in arguing. I hurried then, the sound of a ticking clock pounding in my head. I rushed without running, trusting him that his word was good. Still, I wanted to be as far from that place as my feet could take me before sunrise. I looked back only once, saw the great creatures still looming there, silent. Then, in another instant, like someone had flipped a switch, there was a flash of lightning and a clap of thunder. The rain poured and they vanished before my eyes.

An hour later, I was back on the main road. Neither Goat nor his men dared to follow me that day. But I knew they'd be coming. I made it to the truck just before sunrise. The engine turned over, and I joined the caravan west. Beside me sat the book, its song still echoing in my mind.

I wasn't sure what I would do, but I knew where I would go. My path would not take me back to Somerson. When he'd given me this job, his true motives were not my concern. That didn't seem so obvious anymore. Now I had the book. Perhaps Franklin was right. Perhaps all was lost. And there's no point in fighting destiny. Or maybe, just maybe, this was the key to it all. It would take time, and I would need a place to lie low.

As the rising sun struggled to break through the blanket of clouds, I pulled over to the side of the road. I popped open the glove compartment and pulled out an old, faded map from the days when people still used such things. I spread it out beside me. In a moment I'd found my location and, following the thick lines with my finger, I traced a route to Omaha.

THE GHOST MAP

Gemma Files

Priests and cannibals, prehistoric animals. Everybody happy as the dead come home.
—Shriekback

PEOPLE WITH ONEIROT only have one dream, eventually.

The forest again, rain-misted, loamy. I lie full-length on the dark, moist earth looking up into the green brain cross-section of branches, moss under my head and roots pressing into my ass, my back, so hard I know I'll wake up with bruises. Fresh water dripping into my mouth, leaf-filtered; I can barely see the sky above, just a grey smattering of boiling clouds. It's peaceful. Beautiful. I want to stay here as long as I can.

I know I can't.

I come awake in increments, like always. First the rain stops, then the smell—that firm, verdant smell, so different from my condo's reek of woodsmoke, open cans, unwashed clothes. Then the shifting shadows across my face, my skin, my shut eyelids...they slip away, no matter how hard I try to hold onto them. And when I open them again, when the real world solidifies around me, all that's left are my various aches and pains, phantom or not. The soaked sheets on my bed. The various containers arranged around the room every time I go to sleep, hoping they're just close enough to fill with rain, but not so close I'll kick them over. Fresh water's at a premium, after all; it's like money these days. Back before money was useless, I mean.

There's a stain on my mattress, a stain made from stains. There's a circle of mold growing out of my carpet. And there are spores dug deep in my skin everywhere the dream touched me, which is why I sleep naked these days. For easy access.

The first thing I do when I wake up is set aside the smallest container and wash myself with the cleanest washcloth I still have, the one I only use on me. Then I strop my knife. Then, using what's left of my bathroom mirror, I check for whichever of my growths look readiest for harvest. My daily crop of oneiromantic fungi, growing straight up from my flesh.

The small ones look like blisters, then buds. The large ones curl like mouse ears, dry like jerky, taste like oyster mushrooms. They only bleed a little when you cut them free, and their stems scar over quickly afterward, subdividing at the root. There's one underneath my right breast that's up to five buds per bloom now. Sometimes I wonder how far it'll go before it dies, or I do.

"Meat'shrooms," I call them, mainly because it makes me laugh—and because they're surprisingly good eating, especially when compared with nothing. Of course, my friend Calla Pike didn't find it quite so funny, first time I offered her a bag.

Little too Cronenbergian for me, says Calla. *Nothin' personal, gal.*

Toronto, I point out.

Fair enough, she concedes.

Still, when you think about it (which I obviously do, a lot), auto-cannibalism probably seems like the most economical choice available, contextually. Oh, and did I mention they get you high? Yeah. That's pretty good too, a nice side-benefit. I like having a disease that gives back.

The fungus loves the moisture, as that woman I paid to do my nails used to say, and even with every street outside flooded, I'm still the moistest thing around, I guess, from my spore-laden pores to my gelatinous, membrane-bagged brain. A thousand million neurons firing away in the dark, lit up by a spreading mycelial network. Someday soon I'll be more 'shroom than me, and that'll be great, because at least I won't know what's changed. That I've crossed some point of no return.

At least I hope I won't know. I'd always assumed my neighbour down the hall, the guy with fishpox, crossed that point a while ago, but it's started gnawing at me that I might be wrong.

I call him Bob, when I call him anything—it's probably not his name, but he's never reacted in any way that looks like an objection. I'm pretty sure he's the guy I'd meet sometimes on the way to the mailroom, or coming back from the garbage chute; he always gave me big friendly smiles whenever we shared the elevator, at least until he finally saw Claire and me together... Oh yeah, and I think I remember him smiling again after I got pregnant, because motherhood trumps everything. But I've never been very good with faces. And there isn't much left of his to work with.

Bob comes down the hall every once in a while, clicking with every move he makes, uncertain-gaited and shambling. Only one of his hands still has fingers instead of claws. He taps the doors over and over again, wandering in and out of the empty units, never quite seeming to grasp that he's probably found all the open doors he's ever going to find. When he finds a locked door, he raps on it in the same rhythm every time, repeating the same words with the same intonation, like an mp3 set on repeat: *Can you help me, please? I need help. I'm your neighbour.* The only thing that changes is the underlying timbre of it, which I can hear when he raps on my door. Over the months, it's slowly gotten thicker, more gurgling. Like something viscous and rotten is filling his lungs.

Khhan yu h'llp me, plllss? I nnneed h'lllp... I'm yrrrr neighbourrr.

Used to be I could just shout back, *Fuck off, Bob,* a couple times and get him to move on. But one day about two months ago I made the mistake of looking out my peephole. The hall outside looked empty, and for a moment I thought he'd left, until one sad orange eye extended itself up into my field of view on a long, rubbery stalk. It looked shiny, like it was about to cry. And then came the ever-present rapping and the autonomic pleas for help, sounding like they were right in my head, and I lost it. I screamed through the door: *Jesus Christ, Bob, I didn't want to talk to you when you were just a guy, and I never talked to any of my fucking neighbours anyway! I'm sure as fuck not gonna let you in now!*

And then I'd backed away in sudden, crumpling terror, thinking I'd finally gone too far, that something in him would wake up and realize I'd moved from ambient object to food source or threat, and the next thing I heard would be his claw smashing my door apart, his ruined face appearing in the crack like: *Heeeeeeere's Bobby!*

But nothing happened. I didn't even hear him shambling away. I waited as long as I could before opening the door. On the remains of the rug outside sat something new, something odd: a strip of scaly tissue, translucent and shrinking as it dried. Subsequent visits brought other leavings, like gifts. A molted, hollow claw, sharp enough to cut fabric. Scales that shine in rainbow colours like mosaic glass. A rubbery pearlescent capsule—could be an egg, or an eye-casting, or a piece of excrement for all I know. Other things I can't recognize at all. Not that I try that hard.

Some of them I find uses for. Some of them I just arrange in the corner like art. Sometimes I leave offerings of fresh meat'shrooms outside my door myself; they're always gone by the next day, though I don't know if it's Bob who takes them. *Blind trade*, they called this in an anthro course I took long ago. *A stepping stone for cultural first contact. A critical element in building civilization.*

If something's being built here, I don't know if I want to know what it is.

***

I make the Ghost Map over and over. Update it almost daily. From here to here, safe. From here to here...not so much.

There's a thing over here I call the Drifter, because it pretends to be a waterlogged corpse. Avoid it. It always floats face-up; if you look at it too long, you'll suddenly realize it seems to have the same face—degraded, rotting, fallen slightly in—as one of your loved ones. Whoever it is you most wish you'd been there to die for when the Backsplash came.

(Don't think about Claire. Don't think about Mom. Don't think about Del. Don't think.)

(Don't.)

The Drifter's tethered to something else, farther down, by long ropes of muscle. If you touch it, its arms snap shut and those ropes retract, frog tongue fast, pulling you into the murk. I've never seen the thing below, just what comes up later. It must have sharp jaws, like a clam, or maybe it's a beak, like a squid's. Maybe it extrudes itself up out of some sort of tube, exhales its own guts and grabs you hard with them, then sucks you back inside, where it can digest you slowly. I think I remember hearing about stuff like that—worms, tubes, extremophile life grown on the sides of underwater volcanic vents, in fissures opened in the floors of trenches. Or like those comb jellies with baffled fish stuck inside them, a reel of mucus sacks strung out to form themselves around whatever happens to float by, a line of trawling stomachs. Sometimes you can see the fish start coming apart, still not sure where their scales went, why their flesh is suddenly all on the outside, unprotected, nude. The acids slow-dissolving it layer by layer, spreading it wide in all directions.

(I could look stuff like this up in seconds if my WiFi still worked. If the internet still worked.)

(If anything still worked.)

Or, shit, it occurs to me I used to have a pretty good book on deep-sea life around here, if I haven't burnt it already. But I try not to read much these days, because doing it by firelight gives me a headache and doing it by natural light is difficult unless I want to go up on the roof, which I don't, if I can avoid it. Plus, my books are getting moldy in this humidity, just like everything else, and they stink.

***

They come up out of the water, these things, the same way all of it does. Ever since the pulse, the Backsplash. Ever since—well. You know, I can only assume.

But just in case you don't...

Things got weird, that last year; I didn't notice as much as I should have, but it's not like I was alone in that. Remember what Bruce Cockburn used to sing, about the trouble with normal? I was married to a woman in a wishy-washy country located right above the extremely well-armed one which seemed to be rapidly deciding fascism hadn't really been such a bad idea after all, along with all the homophobic bullshit that entailed, and I'd just had a kid with her too—so, yeah, the things I stayed awake at night worrying about tended to involve reproductive rights and ideological slide with a side-order of climate change paranoia, not whether or not those non-Euclidean nightmares about shoggoths I occasionally had were likely to come true.

Proto-oneirot, that's what it must have been, I now understand. And no, I didn't make up the word; I remember reading it somewhere on the Web, like everything else. People were having the same dreams over and over, and those dreams spread. They looped in other people; they got more palpable. They started to change the waking world.

Yeah, you would *think that, I guess, if it was happening to you,* I remember telling myself, even as it was. *I mean, we all want to believe we're exactly that powerful, don't we? Especially when it makes no difference.*

But as it turns out, those cults we traded smirky memes on Twitter about had a handle on shit after all, didn't they? The Black Woods Thousanders, Dagon's Brood, the Open Door of Night... In the end, we should've all just hitched a ride oceanward and hit the beach too, gone surfing without our boards 'til the riptide sucked us down, on the vain hope our corpses might eventually wash up against Y'ha-nthlei's walls. Or locked ourselves in a warehouse and prayed to Mother Hydra for translocation to the bottom of Monterey Canyon. Six of one, half-dozen of the other.

Still, who even gives a shit at this point?

R'lyeh rose, Cthulhu walked; the ocean floor cracked open, blossoming volcanoes, and the continental shelves began to shift, grinding against each other. Tsunamis rolled in from every angle, flattening coastal areas and flooding things up past the littoral zones. Manhattan sank, sparking an earthquake cascade that humped half of Lake Ontario up and down like a roller coaster, and the Backsplash was the result—I mean, you don't call it a tsunami when a lake's involved, but the effect's basically the same.

The waters rose up, and everything else came with them: Pollution, madness, plague. Fishpox and oneirot. Ghouls forsook their hollows under Mount Pleasant Cemetery and spread southward, drawn by the wet, lapping beat of disaster, the promise of drowned bodies to feast on; deep-sea creatures who shouldn't have been able to sustain the change in pressure without exploding or survive in fresh water nevertheless began to appear in droves, swimming up the channels between buildings. Giant squid with eyes the size of dinner plates, hagfish and wolffish and moray eels hungry for literal blood in the water, coelacanths gesturing with their bony, oddly hinged fins at shell-shocked survivors fishing from buildings' upper floors. Swarms of pike, supposedly locally extinct for more than a hundred years, with their plated tails and dinosaur jaws.

The sun came up bloody through a constant haze of displaced pollutants and dirty rain, while the nights were lit first by fires, then by schools of gigantic, bioluminescent jellyfish eddying upward along the newly carved flood plain—drowned trees and sunken cars, smell of wet, burnt sugar and sour earth under ploughed-up concrete, the former sidewalks twenty feet down at its shallowest points. The slow slope of Bloor Street, pulling itself headlong from Lake Ontario's permanently open, broken-toothed maw.

I figured most of this out in retrospect, of course, same as everybody else who thought worshipping the Old Ones sounded like a hilarious metaphor for...something or other. But I *did*, and long before any asshole with froggy eyes turned up to shout it at me too. I've always been pretty smart that way, when I've had to be.

That's what Claire used to say anyway, even when she was mad at me. Or maybe especially then.

***

Claire was over at Mom's that day, picking up Del on her way home from work. I'd left him there after kindergarten, then gone home to grab a few hours to myself. Wanted to write, but I lay down instead; I was tired still, so tired. Carrying a kid does something to you—well, a lot of things. It doesn't stop with giving birth. You're never quite the same.

Meema time, grandma time. Del loved that. Mom loved him...not *more* than we did, that's a dumb thing to say, but...in a different way. A necessary way. It's good for kids to be loved by as many people as possible, I think.

I hope he's still with her, and Claire. Like, I hope they're still, they're all still—

(fuck)

***

Thirty minutes, walking fast. That's how long it takes to get from our place back to Mom's. How long it took before.

Our building's new. It fronts the lakeshore, right off the water. Lake Ontario at your fingertips. That's how they advertised it on the hoardings, going up. I remember walking by with Claire and Mom before Del was born, watching the construction complete itself in stages, a live-action stop-motion film. *That's where we're going to live,* Claire whispered to me while Mom watched us out of the corner of her eyes, smiling. *That's where we'll bring our kid back to. That's where we'll get old together.*

Cheese, I told her. *Total cheese.*

Cheese can brie a pretty gouda thing though, she replied, deadpan. *You gotta admit.*

Mom's place is smaller, rent-adjusted. We both used to live there, back before Claire and I had even met. It's separated from the lakeshore by the overpass, two levels of highway, but also by a small, double-lane brick tunnel, an underpass running beneath the eastbound GO Train tracks out of Union Station. The same overpass that collapsed when the Backsplash sent an entire trans-oceanic tanker up over the lip of that small harbour next to the sugar processing plant, knocking the unloading crane free and bringing it along for the ride. The water kept on going even when the tanker skewed and slammed slantwise up against the underpass, piling partially crushed concrete chunks and a tangle of unshucked rebar together, like God was playing shitty Tetris, until it formed the world's worst dam.

Then sparks from the grinding wheels set the tanker's venting engine oil on fire, flame and smoke rushing up the slope even as wave after wave kept coming, half garbage, half silt, scraping Lake Ontario's bottom—not clean, exactly, but scraping it. Until their pressure folded the electrical pylons on either side of the tracks first in half, then in quarters, a crumpled newspaper wrapped with wires that only stayed live long enough to kill every fish they came into contact with. And you can just imagine how *that* still smelled a month or so on, when Calla Pike and I rowed over to see if there was any way through...

There wasn't, obviously. Still isn't.

For myself, I came awake blind and shaking when the first wave hit our lobby, breaking out windows from floors two to seven, cracking the rest. Felt the building give one huge heave, the way they always tell you tall buildings do when the winds are high, but far more...blatantly. Heard one of our bookcases fall over against the back of the couch, creating enough space for the rest of them to tip; heard all of Claire's old boardgames come rattling off the last in line's top, scattering dust and cards and counters everywhere.

I didn't even have pants on when I jumped out of bed, not that I noticed until the rain started hitting me, blowing in off the lake so hard it was almost sideways. Didn't have my glasses either, which meant I had to run back in and grab them in order to take stock of the rest in a series of lightning-lit screengrabs, pixilated almost beyond understanding by darkness, storm, sheer incredulity.

That's when I saw that the Toronto Islands, green and pleasant stars of our morning view up to that point, were simply *gone*, along with most of the dockyards—the whole former Cherry Beach expressway, aside from one of those two giant concrete storage tanks and the very top of that annoying fucking waterside dance club whose speakers blasted electronica so loudly across the water every Friday to Sunday you could literally hear the bass in your chest whenever you stepped outside: *Oontz—oontz—oontz—oontz—oontz.* This was worse, and a whole lot less rhythmic.

One wave had already gone by, but another was building; I could tell because the horizon was raising even as I squinted at it, by degrees far more fast than slow, poised and ready to spill free in yet another gush of pure destruction. Here and there, spouts whipped up from the harbour's pockmarked surface as what looked like potential tornado vortices trailed down to meet them, stirring boat wreckage like toothpicks. I saw the upside down hull of a three-masted schooner buck like a mechanical bull, throwing off survivors in every direction; some started swimming frantically the minute they hit the water, while others just clung together and let themselves sink, for which I couldn't blame them. Because—

—there were things *moving* behind the clouds, I now realized, along with everything else. Giant things, awful things, impossible to entirely process. So big they folded almost whole sections of skies around themselves as they lurched and flopped and eddied back and forth, illuminated only in brief sections. Something with a head made from tentacles. Something with eyes peering out from all over the shadows of its rough and slimy body, blinking like REM sleep stars, throwing light back before sucking it back in again and shifting elsewhere, as if searching for prey large enough to merit its attention. Something like a flittering tornadic debris ball whose reflectivity had translated itself from screen life to real life, a living cascade of glowing aerial *things* so wide it tinged the closest lightning strikes with its own particular shades: foul yellow, horrible green, swarming blobby quicksilver.

Their smell made me want to vomit, so I did, but kept on watching; their movements made my hair raise and my sweat run cold, made nausea my default state of being. The mere fact of their existence was so hypnotic, I forgot all about Claire, and Del, and Mom. I forgot about my own safety. I forgot to blink.

Eventually, exhausted by trauma's weight, my eyes rolled back and I folded like a rug, hitting my head so hard I woke up stuck to the carpet.

***

This is the bucket then, slowly heating; we are the frogs, just beginning to cook, to smell our own delicious flesh, the soup we're becoming. Determined to live while we're alive, as fully as possible under the circumstances. To slow things down and feel whatever joy we can until the inevitable. The smell can be sweet, even to you; it can make your mouth water. Remind you of better days, days of plenty. Days of possibility. Days before.

Sometimes I think about the doom-shouters who used to pass by my building at what seemed like the same time every night, each moving past the other in an entirely different direction. One sounded like an enraged dog, snarl-cursing the whole universe in general and every rich asshole with a harbour view in particular, voluble and inventive; the other just screamed out a series of stuttering, inarticulate howls, as if he was venting a lifetime's worth of existential pain. You could set your watch by them, if anybody listening still had a watch instead of a smartphone.

I kind of miss those guys, especially right now—they were reliable at least, and their mutual spectacle oddly made me feel better, especially when I was feeling bad...feeling fear, feeling sadness, feeling doubt. Anything I didn't want to articulate out loud, to trouble Claire with, would simply channel itself through them—squeeze out and away as they faded into the distance, dissolving without a trace, leaving me free to turn cumbersomely and fit my Del-inflated abdomen back to her curves, allow myself to submerge into her welcome warmth. But since they were down there at street-level on Backsplash night, I'm fairly sure I know what happened to them.

Now, without them to vent for me, I just have to keep it all inside. Pretend I feel nothing, until I do.

Back to the grind then. The new grind. Cooking stuff over a fire in the bathtub, using an air-fryer grill balanced atop an extra-deep roasting pan full of charcoal to cobble together a porcelain-set firepit. It's hard to find things to burn when everything's so soggy, but I manage. Oh, and then there's journalling to keep myself sane, for as long as the sun stays up and my pens don't run out of ink. When things get dim, meanwhile, I arm myself with a hammer and hang a hand-cranked flashlamp 'round my neck for the eight-story emergency stairwell climb to our building's roof-garden, hoping to pick a few fresh vegetables, check my nets for birds, raid the garbage tubs I set out for real-life rainwater. Or assemble and re-assemble my go-bag, still unsure where I'm going to go.

On the roof, just past the garden, someone's been building what I guess is a totem—a scare god, something to pray to, so the tomatoes don't come up flyblown. Got a toaster where its head should be, still surprisingly shiny, a bright Ikea job. I never see them add to it, not that I've been looking.

You can avoid other people just as well as ever, I find, these days. Even better, now most of them are dead.

In the beginning, I found trinkets left in front of the totem: necklaces, earrings, silver set with what might've been diamonds or rhinestones. Sort of useless shit the ghat won't even take in trade. Not a lot of call up here for jewelry these days. The gold standard took a dive along with everything else; you can't eat it, after all.

After that came photos of the lost, the missing—unreadable notes to scratched-out faces, gravestones for the drowned. Toys and dolls, dead pets; dead pets Frankensteined together *into* dolls, into toys. Then salvage—batteries, broken tech, leftover meds. Food, even. When people start to give away the stuff they actually need to something which may or may not exist, that's when you know things *must* be bad.

There's a new bowl there now, red-smeared, full of flies. I think it holds fingers, but I haven't looked real close.

Climb and collect, pack and re-pack, scribble 'til dusk. Wash as much skin as I can reach. Lie down in darkness, drift away, then surface in darkness once more, shocked awake by the sound of Bob's feeble claw-knock. Close my eyes by touch alone, knowing damn well the best I can hope for is more of my creeping, deepening oneirot dreams.

And after I wake...

***

So it's a couple days ago—maybe three—and I'm panning for trash down around one of the ghats with Calla Pike, who drives her water taxi past my balcony twice a week or even three times, depending on how lonely she feels. Used to run it back and forth to the Islands with tourists and day-trippers, back when any part of those were still above water; she's from Newfoundland originally, so I guess maybe all this isn't quite as unfamiliar to her as it is to me. Or maybe I'm being provincialist.

One way or the other, I was pretty damn happy to see her the day she came banging on my sliding door with her boat hook, since I'd spent the previous hour or so standing in what used to be my and Claire's kitchen, thinking very seriously about the easiest, least painful way to kill myself, given what I had on hand.

Cut my throat with my sharpest knife? Simple and direct, except I'd have to really punch it through because skin is tougher than it looks, and I also couldn't remember which side my jugular vein was on; botch it, and I'd spend my last minutes in agony. Hang myself prison-style from a door handle? Sure, if I could find something I was reasonably sure wouldn't just break after I blacked out and went slack, because I never did lose those post-pregnancy pounds...and if *that* went wrong, with my luck I'd wake up with just enough brain damage to forget how to survive, but not enough to be able to blissfully ignore dying.

Anyhow, doesn't matter—Calla turned up instead.

Thunderin' Jaysus, woman, tell me ya got a piss bucket empty somewhere in this high-end joint! she'd hollered at me, trying not to tap so hard she cracked the glass. I'd been startled enough to jump, then glance automatically down and lock eyes with her, so she'd grinned at me hopefully, and something about simply being able to smile at another person—hopefully human, hopefully sane—knocked down my every defense.

Sure, I said, finally. *Need a hand, or can you make it up here yourself?*

She snorted, clambering off her raft and onto my balcony, guns popping out grapefruit-sized like she was trying out for a Dave Bautista impersonator drag king contest. Answering, as she did, *Yeah, I think I'm good. 'S just how if ya stick your arse out t' piss in the flood, something's like as not to take it personal and bite it off these days.* Adding, as she ran for my bathroom, *Grab a hold onto my float line there, wouldya? Much obliged. Free trip on me after, for payback.*

I never quite bought into her manic cheer, not then or later on, but even a feigned version of happiness seemed pretty charming from where I'd been sitting, not to mention unutterably superior to the silence of my own head. Which was why having her around made things not perfect, but better...much as they could be, given the circumstances.

Closest ghat-station to me and Calla sits on top of what's left of the sugar processing plant's intake chute-house roof. The trash gets piled on one side, while corpses get laid out to dry on the other, keepers poking both heaps intermittently until they're judged flammable enough to add together on the pyre bowl up top, doused in gas, and flame-throwered back to high heat—greasy smoke and too-sweet stench reaching lazily upward all day long, smudging the crack between clouds where we used to assume heaven might be.

It's a clean city initiative, Metro Toronto City Council-driven, for all the day's ashes get raked into the water below every sunset. Ghat-keepers pay any citizen who turns up once for garbage, twice for human remains, though not in money: MREs and cans, meds and filters, the occasional tool, rainwear cobbled together out of plastic and donated clothing, rubber boots. Every little bit helps, on both sides of the equation.

Around Christmas last year, I swapped one guy a double bag of meat'shrooms and a half-gallon of dream-rain in a container that once held white vinegar from No Frills for three tubes of waterproof caulk, then wrapped them up in a scarf Claire used to like. When I passed the present over to Calla and started humming, "Hark the Herald Angels Sing," she was so moved she almost cried.

Again, anyhow.

Down around the ghat, where Sugar Beach once was, where Calla's water taxi's hull still bumps over the occasional deep-rooted pink sun umbrella, and the submerged tops of willow trees have started to grow together in knots, festooned with algae and lake weed. Back to me and Calla, raking in a fresh load of (at least partly literal) crap, before pausing to note something bigger a bit farther down, maybe snagged under the waterline—maybe bobbing, but not quite floating, or drifting. Where I squint down hard, adjusting for blur, trying my level best to figure out if it's predatory while keeping *just* far enough away to make things hard, if it tries any sort of sneak attack—

Which, naturally enough, is exactly when said thing starts to move faster, dipping steadily upward.

First a shadow, then a ripple, a head breaking surface, eyes bugged out wide and black, made for the deep. I see the membranes flicker first one way and then the other, masking it from daylight, nictitating to keep them moist. Watch the gills on the sides of its—his? No hair, so maybe—neck close up as the thing coughs a bit before telling me, in a husky, air-drowned voice—

"You, we... I. Need to...talk. Dis*cuss*."

I scoff. "Yeah, I don't think so."

"Do, yes. To you."

"Uh, *no*."

"Ya heard her, fish-face," Calla puts in at almost the same time. "Got a wrong 'un, so piss off, and keep on goin'. I mean, I get how we all must look sorta the same t' you, but c'mon—she don't even like men, scales or no scales. Just take the hit, boyo."

But it (he) keeps on staring, unabashed, barnacles dotting his flat yet not completely unattractive face like beauty marks. And when he opens his mouth again, I can see an isopod squatting where his tongue should be, opening its own tiny mouth as if it's channelling that odd voice up from inside itself. Like he's a funnel, a living megaphone.

"To *you*," he repeats, to which I just shrug. Replying—

"Okay then. What's my name?"

"You are...woman."

"Good try, my dude, or whatever. I *am* a woman—we both are. So?"

Another pause; Calla and I glance at each other, trying not to seem amused. "Think fast," she warns him, scooping up a can from the nets—crushed, not full, so it's good for recycling and not much else. Aside from scoring points off the occasional Wet One.

"Wait," he says, head dipping slightly. "You...breathe air. You are—"

"Name, or it doesn't happen, guy."

"—you, hm... I..."

106

"Blow," Calla says, not missing a beat. "*That*'s what yeh bloody do." And lets fly.

The can bounces off, barely making a sound where it impacts against his skin. He slicks his membranes at us once more, water-folk version of the side-eye, and submerges. With not even a dip left behind in his wake, let alone a ripple.

"Yeh need to stop talkin' to them," Calla tells me when he's gone. "Don't know why ya even gave that one the time of day in the first damn place—nothin' good's like t' come of it, tell yeh that much for damn free."

"Probably not," I agree. Then add, after a minute, "Then again, he was the one started talking to *me*."

"Yeah, well. You need to stop answering."

You talked to him too, I manage not to say, before bowing my head and getting back to our mutual business. I mean, it's not like I disagree. Nothing good *is* likely to come of talking to them. But the fact they've started talking at all...that they bothered learning how...

...well, that's interesting. Isn't it?

Might mean something more is going on here than just the usual, the general Ghost Map traps-and-snares jig. Might even mean they want something from us they can't just take, at least...

(not without asking)

Discuss. What, exactly?

I kind of want to know.

Claire used to call that sort of thing leverage, I think to myself—not telling Calla, because I know how she'll react if I do. But also because it still hurts too much to even think Claire's name, let alone to say it, outside of in my dreams.

***

So here I am, peering out the window at a Hieronymous Bosch world. The days trickle by, more entries accumulating. The Ghost Map expands—sidelong and downward only, east by west by south, never north. Never up past the train tracks, the blockages keeping Claire and me apart. Claire, Mom, Del.

What would Claire do, I ask myself over and over, if she was here? Take it all in real small, play it real slow. Let it hurt.

Learn from it.

(Well, I'm trying.)

Aside from the Drifter, there's another thing floats down near what used to be our back gate, the door to the recycling room. It plays dead too, floating slack until people get close enough for it to hug, stinging them all over with a million pixilated tongues, melting them close 'til they get slimy enough to absorb through its skin. It casts a pale light up through grey water, rippling pleasantly, maybe hypnotically. Sometimes I think I can see it reorganizing itself, changing to suit fresh prey. I call it the Bear-Trap, mainly because I can.

Then there's the ghouls—actual ones, corpse-eating and all, dog-snouted, red-eyed. They smell worse than dead Saint Bernards, which I now know for sure, having smelled at least one. Or the shoggoths, which can look like almost anything once they've life-cycled from seed to tuber to animal/mineral/vegetable, but more often than not I seem to spot in mid-growth out of other stuff, stuff they've ingested enough of to begin repurposing. One drowned tree in a stand of drowned trees, reaching up with hands made from silty branches; a clump of fungus and bulbs growing out the side of a burnt-out building, reaching down with vines spun from slime. A wasp's nest the size of two hugging children formed around what used to be a traffic light with a face looking out the bottom and bones spread like sheaf of decay just above it, pumping out scent, trying to tempt carrion birds in close enough to swallow.

Got one of my old folklore books down from a high shelf recently, where it managed to stay mostly dry, and now I amuse myself by finding Japanese yokai-ish names for the things Calla and I see as we cruise around. One morning, something like a moving coral reef breaks the harbour surface between my apartment and where the Islands used to be, something white and jagged and oily-sheened that undulates up and down before submerging; it reminds me of a *bake-kujira*, a "ghost whale," the skeletal whale corpse said to haunt Japanese whaling villages and bring them disease, along with influxes of weird fish (check) and weird birds (no check thus far, but I'm setting my watch).

Hard t'blame 'em, Calla remarks when I tell her. Then, shading her eyes, *Don't look much like a whale though. Too skinny, and that skull's like—what's that thing used to hang in the ROM, out over the staircase? Ix-something?*

Icthyosaur. They used to have a whole display of them back in the day, off in a cavern where the dinosaur exhibit ended, before they got hold of all those Albertosauruses. So, "ghost icthyosaur." Icthy-kujira?

Fuck, I look like I care? Calla snorts, companionably. *Put it down as "big bastard, safe harbour risk." Jaysus, I wonder if that's the actual museum's skeleton,* she goes on a moment later, belying her own supposed disinterest. *Seen weirder shit, I guess...but not by much.*

Five days later, so have I.

I've given in for the first time to Calla's urging to explore northward, after she finally came up with a reason worth the risk: She wants to explore Allan Gardens, the ruins of the conservatory, where there might well still be seed stores worth trading. We've parked the water taxi on Jarvis Street at Gerrard, where the water finally shallowed out enough to walk, then sloshed the rest of the way north on foot. For no reason either of us have ever figured out, the hour just before dawn seems to be when most of the Ghost Map goes dormant; you can do a lot in that time, surprisingly. Against the slowly lightening sky, the silhouette of the Gardens' broken dome towers over piles of fallen trees and urban wreckage. The air's deceptively clear, and quiet.

Then a shattering nails-on-glass scream with the volume of a dozen jet engines physically knocks both me and Calla over, and a gigantic, tentacle-lined worm-like shape the color of tar and neon rears up out of the ruined dome, writhing in frantic spasms that bring down the rest of it in flung shards. We 180 and haul ass out of there faster than I've ever moved in my life, not looking back even once, not stopping until we're back on the water taxi and the taxi's almost all the way back to my place. We collapse on the deck, staring up at the roiling dawn sky, gasping.

Fuck was that? Calla finally manages to gulp.

Name-kujira, I pant. *Ghost slug. Should've known,* I add. *Really.*

What?! Why?

I shrug. *Well...they live in gardens.*

Laughter is a strange sound these days.

***

Up on the roof, a few days later, the finger bowls stand empty, even the rot either picked or washed away. That's another religion down the drain, I think.

Stand squinting over the edge, horizon too hazed for detail, thinking about ticking clocks—how Toronto's finished, at least down here, and what I've cobbled together can't possibly last much longer; it's just not *safe*, and can't be made so, ever. How probably nowhere is, but Canada's still a damn big place, if I can only get myself as far away from its edges as seems feasible. Anywhere not immediately adjacent to water, that would be the goal...

Then making my way back down to my own floor, ears peeled for Bob, but hearing nothing. Not a click, not a shamble, not a moaning plea. Thinking maybe he's so grown-together now he can't move anymore, or maybe he's just sick of the rejection.

I remember how I opened the door a week or so back, carefully, only to find he'd left an almost-complete molt-shell of himself propped up next to my sill, leaning slightly back against the corridor wall. I took it inside, examining it closely: so light yet hard, impossible to chip or break, even with a hammer. I realized I could slip it on in sections, like a suit of armour, so long as I took care to muffle myself enough underneath—the world's weirdest, not to mention stinkiest, set of protective gear. Visibility through Bob's head-helmet was for shit, but the smell alone might keep the things off me while I surfed the lower floors' floodwaters for anything other scavengers might have missed.

Was it a gift? I wondered. Some sort of cross-species courtship token? Must've taken time to put together, if nothing else. And he'd done it so atypically quietly too.

Next morning I left a whole bag of meat'shrooms outside with a sheet of paper folded up next to it, over which I'd scribbled: BOB—THANKS FOR THE SHELL. THESE WILL HELP.

(*might* help)

(hopefully)

Well, turnabout *is* fair play, or whatever. And it wasn't like I had much else to give away at this point.

***

I'm not sure who I'm writing this for exactly, it sometimes occurs to me. I mean...bad as things are, as they continue, it's not like my story's *over*.

Yet.

***

"Why'd yeh stay exactly?" Calla asks, sitting around in my living room. I cook for her sometimes; sometimes she stays over. It doesn't mean anything.

(I'm not going to let it mean anything.)

I just laugh again—not so heartily, this time.

"Because this is home," I tell her. "Because I didn't have a car, let alone a boat. Hell, I can't even drive. Because I'd just given birth, and I want to see him again sometime. You'd have stayed too; don't pretend you wouldn't." I push myself upright. "For fuck's sake, you *did* stay. Tell me why."

Calla shrugs, the way she does when she wants to pretend she's not bothered. "'Cause I couldn't get out fast enough...and 'cause no matter how bad it gets here, it's still more interesting than th' village. Not like I could taxi all the way back to the Rock, anyway." Adding after a second, more soberly, "And 'cause what I'm doing here helps people. You, the ghat-keepers, other squatters...feels like I matter here. Maybe all the more so, 'cause so many folk think nothin' does anymore."

She pauses, squares her shoulders. "Those 'shrooms of yours— been thinkin' it might be worth broadenin' my horizons. Got any to spare?" She bounces to her feet and goes to my cupboards, not waiting for permission. "Could use a decent trip, I'll tell yeh..."

Makes the mistake of reaching up to the top shelf to look then, which pulls her shirt just far enough out of her pants to show her lower back, and freezes. Maybe she heard me gasp, or maybe she just knew—god knows, I already had a feeling. *You want to tell me something so bad, you need to be high enough to do it.*

"Shit," she says, slumping.

It takes me a minute to find the right words. "When...when did you..."

"Two weeks, I think. Hard to tell back there." She pulls her shirt down over the scaly growths pockmarking her back and turns, folding her arms. "Dreams are gettin' worse too, but whose ain't? I didn't see the point in cryin'. Not like we're not all of us livin' on borrowed time now, eh? And who knows, maybe I'll be the first acquires immunity. Somebody's gotta be."

I push my fist into my throat, stifling what wants to come up. I don't want to think about what fishpox will do to Calla; hunch her over, turn her skin to crusted seeping scales and her eyes to giant blind white orbs, dissolve all her manic mirth and sharp tongue away til she's a shambling, mindless thing like Bob.

Which, I suppose, explains why she doesn't want to think about it either.

"Sure," I rasp, at last. "Least I can do."

***

We share a whole crop. The buzz is amazing and overwhelms her almost immediately; I have a better tolerance. Bounty of my flesh, right? Take, eat. My body and my blood. Hope you like side effects, Calla.

Let her doze off, then I take her boat and find my way down to the lakeshore after she's blissfully oblivious, still high enough not to have any room left in my brain for fear. I navigate my way through the falling light like it's rain, enjoying the way it feels on my skin, playing it with gestures like a world-sized theremin. There was a guy who once hooked a synthesizer up to a fungus network, I vaguely remember, letting the electric charges of the mycelial web produce a weird kind of music. I wonder if that's anything like what I'm hearing now.

At the shore, where the ghat-folk come to meet us sometimes, I splash the water with my bare foot, hoping to attract attention. Shouting as I do, between giggles, "Hey! Fish-boy! You wanted to talk? Here I am! Come on!"

It echoes over the water. No one left to complain I'm too loud. No one interested enough to bother.

"Come on, Fish-face! C'mere! Come—!"

They burst out of the oily water without warning, half a dozen of them, shiny and slick. I scream and lurch backward, falling on my ass, still laughing. Black eyes staring at me like a shark, finned ears flicking drops of water from them.

I can't tell which is the one that spoke to me. Can't even tell if the one that speaks is the same one that did last time.

"You are...woman," says the second from the right.

"And you're whatever the fuck *you* are," I shoot back. "You wanted to talk? Talk. But I want something from you first."

They blink like this makes no sense to them. I don't give them time to think. "There's this disease," I tell them. "Turns us into something like you, some fucked-up mix of you and us. Is there a cure? Any way to stop it, slow it down? Reverse it?"

Still no response.

Tell me, you fuckers! I think, throat contracting on the scream that wants to force its way out—but I'm no doom-shouter, not yet. *Tell* me!

"You...can hear," says the thing eventually. For some reason it lifts a taloned, webbed hand not to its ears, but to its forehead. "You must stop...not listening. Then we help."

I gape. "The fuck does *that* mean? What the—no, wait, *wait!*"

But they've already flipped and dived, like eels, gone with barely a ripple. I scream after them, wordlessly, and then collapse to my knees and onto my face. I can't even sob.

The light feels like razors on my back.

***

That night, I finally dream I see Claire, not just hear her. And Del. Not Mom; I don't know what that means. I don't know if I want to know.

We thought you were dead, she tells me, smiling—not with joy or hysteria, more like she's remembering an old but still funny joke. Del huddles into her lap and stares at me, not saying anything. We're sitting in the condo, which looks exactly the way it used to, but I can't seem to focus on them...like TikTok filters are blurring in and out atop their faces, their bodies; one moment they're normal, the next silver-scaled and naked with red lines down their throats; the next, rotting grey-green husks of themselves, showing yellow bones through black-rimmed wounds. *The really funny thing is, though...you sort of are, aren't you? At least as long as you've stopped moving.*

This brings on the anger I'd almost forgotten, the hot red rage I thought I'd left behind in high school, back when it was the only defense I had—back when feeling alone in an alien world was something all the therapists and counselors told me was *my* problem.

I stayed for you, I tell her carefully, through teeth clenched so hard it hurts. *For both of you.*

Claire nods agreeably. *Hope was half of it,* she says. *But fear was the other half, and there's no point lying now, babe. Fear's been most of it for a while, hasn't it? Fear of never finding us. Of what you'd find if you did. Fear of everything out there—the Ghost Map, scavenger gangs, even some stupid fucking accident like falling on a piece of rebar, right? Not that it hasn't taken guts to stay alive too. Believe me, I see that. Don't think I don't.*

Knowing me well enough, as ever, to know just when to switch from pushy to conciliatory. Tears sting my eyes, even through the rage. My hands clench uselessly, in and out, in and out. *But you need to make a choice, sweetie,* she goes on, inexorable as the Backsplash itself. *Because doing nothing isn't an option anymore. Not for either of you.*

Me and Calla?

You love her. More than us now.

No I don't, I protest automatically. *It's not like that. Not at all.* But she only looks at me, and I have to add, *Not* like you.

Ah ha.

Oh, fuck off, woman, I think, but don't say, though she keeps on smiling anyhow. *And definitely not* more. *Fuck that bullshit.*

Then what will you do to get to us?

Whatever I have to! It's a shout, anger-raw. *Anything! Everything!*

I want my wife back.

I want my son back.

I want to know if my mom is alive or dead.

I want my friend not to turn into a monster.

I want the world back the way it used to be.

I want to stop...fucking *wanting.*

And then I'm kneeling on the rug with my face in my hands, sobbing. The carpet—firm, scratchy, *dry* as a pine-forest floor—scrapes my knees. Saying out loud, as it does, *But I don't...fucking know...how to do it.*

Yes you do. Claire's voice is so unexpectedly close and clear I jolt upright, startled. Her arm snakes around me, her mouth pressed to my ear. Del's forehead rests against mine, smelling of sweaty boy-skin and potato-chip breath. *You just need to listen. Stop shutting us out, and* listen.

(Like this.)

A final smile, so sweet, and she drives her thumbnail down hard, right into my forehead. Bone crunches. Hot viscous liquid bursts down my face. The world goes red.

I scream.

***

I wake.

***

Wake up on the boat again, though I barely remember going out on it. I'm naked, clothes piled underneath me like I thought they made for a better bed than exposed decking, wearing Calla's raincoat for a sheet. It's cold and misty, curdled cream off-white air dense and moist in that just-stopped, can't-decide-if-it's-going-to-start-again way Toronto's always had, apocalypse or no. My hand goes instinctively to my forehead, flinching away once more as the fingerpads bounce off rubbery lumps; I cringe, hunching up and shivering, barely able to make myself move. Everything hurts. Nothing works, and I don't understand why.

I'm out in the harbour, farther than I ever thought I'd go, especially without Calla—the lake, the *bay*, as persnickety asshats used to point out (*bay* applies only to the water between the Islands and the shore; the *lake* is everything else). Like it ever fucking mattered.

I itch all over, backs of my hands set crawling. This can't be good.

Slowly, I unroll myself and inch to the raft's edge. Look down into water just oily-still enough to reflect at least a bit of what I need to know, while I let my hands tell me the rest. Don't know how long I slept, but it was obviously long—and wet—enough to bring on a harvest of meat'shrooms like none I've ever grown before. It looks like I'm wearing a bodystocking of white-marbled foam, streaked with startling flashes of iridescent colour: green, orange, magenta, all

115

sickeningly pliant to the touch. Half my face is covered, though not the half with eyes. For a moment, I want to throw up.

Then the wind shifts. Without warning, I can smell myself. And suddenly...

...I'm *starving*.

Before I know it, I'm ripping great swathes of the fungus off myself, stuffing it down my throat like a jackal tearing carrion meat from a corpse. It tastes like the fresh-baked bread I wasn't able to eat for years before the Backsplash, like icewine straight out of the freezer, like steak seared raw and bloody, and it sings in my gut and my bowels, better than orgasm. I can feel the waves of it going through me. Rewriting me from the inside. Melting me down, like a caterpillar does inside its chrysalis.

What's left of my brain tells me quite calmly that I ought to be afraid. But I can't. I only slump down, finally too full to eat more, breathing slow and shallow, staring at the sky. My skin tingles, ripples, clenches in strange places. For the first time, the moving shapes overhead, far above the clouds, don't look horrifying. They look natural. Fascinating.

A faint splash of water, and a face rises over mine, looking down. Black eyes close briefly beneath the sideways membrane. Its scaly throat vibrates. I can hear it now, for the first time, my eardrums and ear bones adjusted for an ultrasonic sensitivity; it's not human language, but somehow that doesn't matter. *You will be ready,* it says. *Soon.*

"For what?" I whisper back.

To come down. A clawed finger strokes the side of my neck, sliding into grooves that weren't there a few minutes before. *When you feel the cold...here...come down. We will be waiting.*

It sinks back into the water, vanishing. And something like thirty or forty minutes later, when the grooves in my neck have opened to reveal wet red membranes and I can taste the water in my chest, I roll off the raft—

—and dive, downward, after it.

***

I think it's the same day when I climb out of the water back into my condo, but I can't be sure. That's not as important as it used to be anyway. Far less important than the melon-sized pod I'm clutching under one arm. I'm no longer cold, and the lack of clothes doesn't bother me anymore. I pause to look at my reflection in my sliding glass door, mildly intrigued.

I still look mostly like me, although my eyes are larger, and I'm...not thinner, exactly, but more streamlined, like the change has tightened things up, rearranged them. You have to look close to see the gill grooves, closed now. The tough, rubbery membranes between my fingers are almost translucent, similarly hard to see at anything but close range. My eyes hurt briefly as their new internal structure readjusts to see through air instead of water, but then I can see as well as I ever did—better, actually. I grin despite myself.

"Holy shit," husks a raw voice. Leaning unsteadily in the bathroom doorway, Calla stares at me, mouth open, face pale, eyes bulging; one's cataracted over into a yellow-white orb, like ivory. She's wrapped a sheet around her, but it can't hide the splotches of blood all over her body where she's cut away the growths of the fishpox as it progressed. Must've hurt like a motherfucker. "Is that... Fuck, gal, is that *you?*"

I shrug; good question, I guess. What *am* I now? She's never seen anything like me before, that's for certain. Neither have I.

We're just going to have to live with that, the both of us, 'til we can't anymore.

This is where a bit of simple human speech would help though, probably—old-school language, made for above-water ears. Good thing I still have access to it.

So—

I cough, spit, clearing the water out of my throat with a gurgle. And, "Sorry, Cal," I say, words only slightly blurred. "We needed help... Well, you more than me, but even so. This was the only way to get it."

She's shaking where she stands. I belatedly remember that that probably means she's frightened. "What the fuck kind of fuckin' *help*—" she manages to get out, but can't finish.

I pat the pod under my arm, which squelches.

"It's a catalyst," I tell her. "All the shit we've seen so far, that's been, like, prototype runs. They finally worked out a version that still leaves us as...well, as mostly *us*, so to speak. Problem was it was kind of a catch-22—they needed a living host to bond to the catalyst medium, but they couldn't get the medium out into the air to us without it drying out first. I'm just the first one finally listened enough to follow instructions, so I could survive getting down there. And...here I am. Human 2.0."

"But..."

"It's this or Bob, Calla."

A long breath follows—in, then held. Then out again, like a liquid sigh.

"Huh, yeah," she says to herself. "Fuckin' Bob."

"Fuckin' Bob," I agree.

(That poor bastard.)

Rain and stink, sodden paper and burnt furniture, the rising tide of mold. I feel this apartment tighten 'round me like a prison, a cocoon made from detritus, obsolete artifacts of dead futures. Dream-Claire was right, no matter whether or not I just made her up to tell me so; I have to shake free of it. It's time.

Come and find us, love.

Oneirot dreams reaching out, touching each other, melding into one big fantasy, indistinguishable from this awful thing we call "real life." Might be a lie; probably is. Might also be a way to trick myself back into hope though—me, and Calla too.

"Want to meet my family?" I ask her.

There's another pause, even longer. I hold out the pod. Just keep on holding it out, steady but silent, until—at last—she takes it. Weighs it in her hand, soft and shiny, bright with alien life: Something new, or very, very old. The only thing on offer.

"You're gonna have to show me what to do," she says finally.

"Of course," I reply.

And I will. Her, Claire, Del...I'll show everyone. Now I can. Everyone who'll let me.

***

That's the dream.

CLAVIS PERFECTUM
A PRELUDE

William Holloway

This story is dedicated to the memory of Todd Fujawa.

"SOLICITATION OF PROSTITUTION and possession of two controlled substances." It was a statement, posed as a question, or maybe a question posed as a statement, but Nicolas Jobim didn't have an answer.

So he didn't say anything. The man sitting across the desk from him wasn't looking at him anyway. He was fixated on trying to roll a cigarette, and failing miserably. The man looked up at him and stated, "I'm a clean-cut Willie man, not a long-haired Willie kinda guy."

Nicolas cleared his throat and stammered, "Oh, uhhh, okay."

The man—Sheriff Jacob Laramie, from the nameplate on his desk—looked at him and scoffed. He looked back down to the task in front of him. The cigarette paper split and the tobacco fell out.

Laramie sighed, exhaled, and shook his head. "I'm trying to quit, so instead of buying a pack I make myself roll one of these bastards. Therefore I spend all day working just to smoke one damn cigarette."

He grinned. He had kind, watery blue eyes and prematurely white hair, but appeared an otherwise vigorous man, despite the yellowed teeth and fingers.

He nodded. "You don't look like a *Nicolas*. More like a Steve. Maybe a Jeremy...or a Todd."

Nicolas was petrified, but a hint of anger rose to the surface. "I shouldn't be talking to you. I haven't spoken to an attorney."

Laramie leaned back in his old wooden rolling chair and put his hands behind his head. "Well, old Terry Jones is here for Jenny. You should probably talk to him. I'm sure he'll stick his head in in a few minutes."

Nicolas began to stand.

"Sit, junior."

Nicolas sat.

Laramie balanced on his chair. "Jenny is a local girl. Goes by Sapphire or Chanel, or a half-dozen other handles on the websites. She's been hooked since she was a little girl."

Nicolas started, "I didn't know anything about that, I just made a mistake."

Laramie nodded, then swung his legs down and his boots clapped on the wooden floor. "Did you bring her that dope?"

Sweat prickled Nicolas' hairline. "No! I just went over there to..."

"Get your dick sucked." Laramie finished the lie with the truth.

Nicolas' breath came out hard. "I can't say anymore 'til I talk to a lawyer."

"Can you roll a cigarette for me?"

"Uh... Should I just..."

Laramie slid a pouch of tobacco and a package of rolling papers across the desk.

"Whatever you're gonna do, you're gonna roll me a smoke first."

Nicolas closed his eyes tight and a tremor of fear passed through his body. A little sob escaped, but he held back the tears.

He opened his eyes to Laramie appraising him. His own eyes drifted to the little office around him. It was exactly what he thought a small-town sheriff's office in Texas would look like. Brown wood paneling. Long leaf pine floors. Football trophies from the glory days of Sheriff Laramie's youth. Framed pictures of the man with George W. Bush. Barbecue cartons in the trash can. A lingering smell of cigarette smoke. Gun racks and deer heads.

Stuffed pheasants on the desk and Louis L'Amour books on the shelves.

Bluebonnets in a vase that turned out to be an old spittoon.

He leaned forward and started rolling. "I didn't bring drugs to Cleo... I mean Jenny. I didn't know she had them in there."

Laramie nodded and pulled a plastic evidence bag from behind the desk and poured out Nicolas' wallet onto the desk. He opened it and pulled out his driver's license and school IDs.

Laramie ignored the driver's license and went for the IDs. "UT. Adjunct Professor of Ancient Languages *Jobim*. Austin Community College. Spanish teacher."

Nicolas replied, barely above a whisper, "Sometimes philosophy, sometimes political science, it just depends on what they need."

Laramie shook his head and his brows furrowed. "Ancient languages. What's that?"

Nicolas couldn't get a read on Laramie. Why would this guy care?

"Dead languages, things people don't speak anymore. Mostly Aramaic, which is what Christ would've spoken, but also ancient forms of Latin, Greek, Hebrew, and Arabic..."

He trailed off. Something about this was off. He wanted to shut up, to wait for a lawyer, but he was also afraid of looking guilty. He didn't know what to do.

Laramie gazed at him and shook his head. "Well, look at the big brain on *Nicolas*."

He let that hang in the air for a moment. "While you were in the holding cell, I called a friend in DPS. Campus Police in Austin are DPS."

Nicolas looked at the floor and shook his head, his black locks framing his face. He was handsome in a boyish, bookish way.

He asked, bitterness hard to hide, "So, did you hear any good gossip?"

Laramie leaned back again and looked up at the ceiling. "You know, the Longhorns. But oddly enough, the subject of one Nicolas Jobim did happen to come up."

Nicolas placed the newly rolled cigarette on the desk and stared straight at the floor. Laramie continued. "Long story short, it turns out the *allegations* were that of a despondent, lovestruck coed. Jilted. She felt used, so she made up some things about a teacher. He got cleared, but the investigation turned up a regular bunny hutch of nineteen to twenty-one-year-old girls with straight A's."

The silence hung suspended until the thrum of the air conditioner filled in the empty spaces.

Laramie cleared his throat. He reached across the desk for the cigarette. He leaned back in his chair again and put his boots up on the desk. Fished a lighter out of his pocket. Placed the cigarette to his lips and lit up. "Nothing finer. Nothing."

He glanced over to Nicolas. "So my friend in the DPS theorizes—" He stopped, mid thought. "That's what you guys do, right? You theorize?"

Nicolas nodded, but didn't look up. Laramie kept going. "So my friend theorizes that you came here to clear you head of distractions to work on your thesis. Make ends meet teaching Spanish at the community college. Something like that?"

Nicolas nodded. "Yeah."

Laramie guffawed. "But I guess separation from all that fine young ass caused a few errors in judgment?"

Nicolas glanced up, but kept it shut.

Laramie craned his neck to look out the open door of the office into the station. "Pendleton! Bring that box in here, would ya?"

He turned his head back to Nicolas and his gaze took on a harder edge. "So I saw you looking around the office. Taking it all in. Wondering, *What kind of hick town shitstorm have I done stepped in? Deer heads and gun racks, for God's sake!*"

They were interrupted by a tired young deputy huffing and puffing a big box through the door and placing it none too gently on Laramie's desk.

Laramie gazed over the top of the box at Nicolas and pulled an old tome off the top of the books in the box.

Without looking up from the book, he asked. "So, Nicolas Jobim. Professor of big, very important thoughts. Irresistible to the nubile undergraduates of Austin, Texas. I've got a question for you."

"I'm an academic. I have a doctorate in..." He stuttered and stopped.

Laramie opened the book and started reading the first page. "So, Nicolas, in your mind, *who* do you think looks to *my* mind like a commie pervert?"

Nicolas inhaled sharply. His breathing came quickly in and out.

Laramie nodded, closed the book, and read the title. "*Theatricum Chemicum Brittanicum.*"

He reached down into the box for another. "*De Nigromancia, or, Concerning the Black Arte.*"

And another. "*The Malleus Malificarum* and *The Picatrix.*"

He looked up and raised his eyebrows. "You have a fascinating library, Professor Jobim."

Nicolas stammered, "It's for my thesis."

Laramie asked, "I'll bet they are! What's your thesis about?"

Nicolas' stammering became stuttering. "Um, I haven't fully theorized...but...but...it's about the translation of medieval grimoires and original source materials and whether they—"

Laramie interrupted, "So would you consider yourself an expert or even an authority on the topic?"

Nicolas stared at the man, agape like a fish out of water.

"Just nod if yes. Because you're studying this for your thesis and not because you're a pervert here to start a cult or sacrifice children. Right?"

"What?"

"Have you ever seen that movie about those teenagers in Arkansas accused of murdering those little kids because they were into devil worship? The West Memphis Three? They ended up going to prison for *years*, and the only evidence was that they listened to heavy metal and wore black clothes."

"Uhh..." That was all Nicolas could manage. A single tear slid down his cheek.

Laramie stood and walked around his desk, then closed the door, banishing the noise of the office outside.

"I hear the DA for our little county is going to be making an appearance. I wouldn't want him to barge in on our little heart to heart here. You wouldn't want that, would you? He's a Bible thumper, that one. Lock em' up and throw away the key."

He put a hand on Nicolas' shoulder and sat down on the desk in front of him. "Nicolas, I don't want a guy like that seeing a box of books like these, I really don't. But I'll bet half the guys in the office out there were going through these. Showing them to the secretary. Calling their ministers, warning them about the deviant sitting in the office with the sheriff this very minute."

He let that thought percolate in Nicolas' head. "You wouldn't want that either, would you, Nicolas?"

Nicolas shook his head back and forth.

"Son, you're what? Early thirties?"

Nicolas nodded.

"Pretty, if I may say, boyish. Not really all that tough looking. You got that Silicon Valley look. You know, where they're billionaires but they wear those zipper sweatshirts all the time? Skinny, glasses. The penitentiary is gonna be hard on you, I can't lie, son."

Tears now colored the front of Nicolas' shirt.

"So, son, tell me. Is your interest in these books merely academic, and if so, would you consider yourself an expert on the topic?"

Nicolas nodded as the tears flowed. "Yes, I'm just a stupid academic, I just made a mistake."

"And as an academic, are you an expert on this topic?"

"Yeah, probably, as best as I can tell."

"Good, son, then I'm going to hold off on referring you to the district attorney on drug distribution charges for now, and I'm going to keep this box under my desk provided that you and I have an agreement."

"Yes, anything, I swear, anything. What do I have to do?"

"I'm going to drive you home. Then I'm going to pick you up in the morning and tell you a story you're going to wish you never heard. Now get yourself together, you're going home."

Headlights backlit the blinds in Sheriff Laramie's office and fell across Nicolas' tearful face. Laramie turned around and peeked through the wood-colored blinds.

He glanced up and over to Nicolas. "Okay, are you gonna hold it together? That's him, the DA. You and I need stand up, walk through that door, go through the office and out those front doors. We need to do that before he comes through the back door, or your situation goes from bad to worse."

He stood and hefted the box of books up and under his desk.

"On your feet, junior, it's go time."

Nicolas stared like the proverbial deer in headlights.

Laramie sighed. "You got all sort of instincts, boy, but self-preservation ain't one of them. Get on your fucking feet."

Nicolas' breath caught in a sharp inhale and he practically leapt to his feet.

"Good boy," chuckled Laramie.

He walked over and put his hand on Nicolas' shoulder and turned him around. He grabbed his other arm, and in one motion the cuffs were on the frightened young teacher.

Laramie pushed him forward through the door of the office. "Don't forget where you are and that your actions from this point forward determine who you're gonna be for the rest of your life. Now, we're gonna walk through this office and you're gonna look at the ground in front of you."

They walked through the doors to the busy office. Cleo-Sapphire-Jenny sat handcuffed at a desk talking to a young uniformed deputy. Whore makeup smeared, eyes twitching, bleach blonde hair in a riot of tangles. She glanced up at Nicolas, then quickly away.

Other deputies looked up at them. Secretaries too. Even the janitor.

Guilty. Pervert. Weirdo.

Arresting a John coming out of the love shack isn't all that interesting.

But he sure did have an interesting book collection, didn't he?

Nicolas walked, the skin of his face flushed, trembling and tear-stricken, out through the front door.

"To the right, junior. Let's get around the corner and make sure your new best friend isn't waiting for us in the parking lot. He thinks I'm too soft on the weirdos and perverts that the Austin liberals grow like geraniums. He probably figured I'd sneak you out before he got there to throw the book at you."

Nicolas stammered. "Thank you. I'm so sorry. I never would have..."

They rounded the corner and Laramie said, "Save it. You're not in the clear, kid."

Nicolas and Laramie rounded the corner to the back parking lot and Laramie pulled up short and took a quick peek. "Okay, he's not back here. Not sitting in his car. We must've timed it just right."

He pushed Nicolas over to a grey-silver Crown Victoria, opened the passenger door, and pushed him in. He got in the driver's side, and pulled them out and away into the night.

Margaret gave him a funny look while pulling out of their shared driveway. Caked on makeup and a pant suit; a cubicle at H&R Block. Nicolas lived in a nondescript brown townhouse. Had his arrest last night rendered him something other than an adjunct professor of this and that? Was he no longer a nondescript-brown kinda guy in Margaret's book? Had a small-town gossip machine fed all the details to her while he sat in the holding cell?

She pulled away as Laramie pulled up in his nondescript Crown Vic.

Nic got in, looking forward, no eye contact with Laramie. He muttered something about a good morning, but Laramie didn't put it in reverse and take him to the morning encounter that he'd mentioned when he dropped him off at 3 AM.

"Take of your sunglasses and look at me, kid."

Nic cleared his throat, nodded, and took off his imitation Wayfarers. He nodded again and looked at Laramie.

The sheriff's watery blue eyes searched his and he took a deep breath. "I didn't sleep much last night."

Laramie grinned and put it in reverse, pulled out, then put it into drive to take them to their destination. "Well, I imagine you had a few things on your mind. The future, that sort of thing, no?"

Nic closes his eyes and felt grit beneath his lids. He put the imitation Wayfarers back on. They turned away from downtown Smithville and out toward the highway, but pulled up short into the old self-storage facility on the side of the farm road. Laramie got out, unlocked the dilapidated old gate, then returned and drove them through.

"The city and county bought this place when the owner, old Joe Kerrick, kicked the bucket about twenty years back. He hadn't paid taxes for years and had no kids to speak of, so the county opted for this place instead of shelling out for a brand-new building."

Nic's mind was elsewhere, so he said nothing as Laramie pulled up to a storage space, got out, unlocked the door and raised it, revealing old cardboard boxes as far as the eye could see.

He seemed to know exactly what he was looking for as he squatted down and hefted one out to the car. He opened the trunk, dropped it in, closed it, and got in the driver's side.

He pulled out a dented old thermos and two tin cups, pouring a steaming stream into one and the next, then handed the next to Nic. He didn't say anything, just sipped his coffee and stared out to the morning sky, blue and cloudless.

Nic took a sip. Pretty good. He took off his imitation Wayfarers and looked at his eyes in the mirror. Puffy, exhausted, ringed in red and purple. "Do you actually need my help with something, or did you just...want to let me off the hook for what happened last night?"

Laramie paused. "I'm not letting you off the hook for last night. Nothing *happened* last night. You broke the law. You exploited a little girl I watched grow up in this little town. Trailer to trailer to juvie to jail. Never had a chance. So, no, I'm not letting you off the hook."

They sat for an ugly moment and Laramie continued. "I don't like you, Nicolas. You're a bad person no matter how you slice it. Not a bad person that's gonna hold up a gas station, but a bad person nonetheless."

A little shiver passed through Nicolas' heart. *I'm not a bad person.* He didn't say anything, but the void inside of him grew wider.

He cleared his throat. Delicate now. "I made a mistake and..."

He stopped talking. Somehow the euphemisms and rationalizations that formed the constellations of his life seemed a lot more euphemistic and a lot less rational.

Laramie took his hands off the steering wheel and looked at them. Old, sun-weathered and tough, but his eyes settled on the simple thin gold wedding band on his left.

"So tell me, Nic, have you ever seen something that wasn't supposed to be there, something that wasn't supposed to happen?"

Somehow a bitter little smile cracked Nic's face.

He nodded.

"I'd been a cop for a little then, and a married man for a little while longer. Silly, you know, high school sweethearts in a small town, but that's what happened. Raised a few eyebrows back then though.

Her name was Janelle and she's from here too. She was black and I was white, and there was no love between black and... Well, I suppose it's a familiar story. We'd put away several of her family members through the years, most likely for nothing at all.

This would've been the late 1980s, but in certain small-town ways, it might as well've been 1880.

That's when the big oil bust happened and the economy for a lot of towns like this went to shit, so when Nelson Garvey buys a big piece of dirt and construction workers get jobs, nobody raises an eye...like they did when the son of the chief of police married a black girl, but that's another story.

It took several years to build that place, and it was odd. He'd have parts built, then immediately have them torn down. No expense spared. They must've laid in that slab four times before he was satisfied. And the finished product made no sense.

It was a strange-looking place, even though the men who built it were the only ones to see it. It's set back from the road about a quarter mile into the woods, and it looks like it was laid out...like he was more interested in symmetry than anything functional.

But then it was finished, the workers went home, and it was forgotten 'til one day someone realized we hadn't seen Nelson Garvey in more than a year. Maybe longer. Then someone told that Nelson had hired *Worm* as his groundskeeper.

See, almost everybody in a small town gets a nickname by the locals. Most them just call me Chief. Maybe they got something more clever than that, but don't mention it to a guy whose primary handle is Chief. A bit of caution perhaps. They'll probably give you one too, probably something about your little faux pas last night. It's hardly ever flattering.

But I digress. *Worm.*

Bartholemew Anderson is his real name. Don't want to be a gossip about what his name refers to because it isn't important. But you can use your imagination.

Well, Worm killed a trespasser. Then he called us up.

And that was the highlight of the 90's for the Smithville PD. We got there and every little thing was weirder than the next. That house. Good Lord. It's hard to look at.

Jesus.

Okay, Nelson Garvey was a New York investor of some sort. Lost more in the oil bust than ten of you or me will make in ten lifetimes. Apparently still had more money than God because he retired from there and moved here and built that house.

Why here? No idea.

Then, somehow, somebody that rich hires a worm like Worm and disappears, leaving Worm as the groundskeeper with an escrow account to keep the place up. To keep electricity out to the place. And a phone line.

So no one ever told you about Worm? Only old farts like me remember him. Most people have never seen him, and never will. He lives back in the woods in a little barn outside the house. It looked like he hadn't been inside the house for...years before he called us two weeks ago.

This would've been his 4th call to us since the 90s. Since Nelson Garvey got here, built a house that made no sense, and disappeared.

And every time Worm calls us, it's because he's killed someone. That makes it about one per decade since they built that house. It's always a trespasser.

Well, I guess I will tell you a thing or two about Worm... After that first time he called us and we went out there to conduct an investigation, and you gotta know this: we *wanted* to put Worm away for that. We did. He shot that guy with a deer rifle with no warning. From the footprints, he had no idea Worm was even there.

But the guy was armed, and he was trespassing. He had a little .380 and a knife.

I'll tell you a bit more about that trespasser—and the other trespassers—later.

Well, a few months later, one of the antique shops called us up saying Worm had been by selling some things. Not a huge amount of money. Well, one of the folks they sold that little *object d' arte* to came back and told them they got it appraised and that it was really, really valuable. It was from some foofy New York artist and cost more than a house.

So we wanted to arrest Worm, but nothing stuck because we couldn't prove anything. There weren't cameras everywhere back then, and we couldn't prove he'd gotten it from Garvey's mansion.

Well, one of the other things he sold is in that box in the back seat.

Let's go back to your place, I'm pretty sure you'll find this pretty interesting."

Laramie and Nic pulled back into the driveway of Nic's little townhouse. Laramie put it in park and shut it off, and his hand went to the door handle, but he noticed Nic wasn't moving. He stared straight ahead, lip quivering.

"When all of this...all of this...whatever it is...is over..." He trailed off.

Laramie sat back in his seat and fixed the younger man in his gaze.

"What's on your mind, Nic?"

Nic paused, his breath coming in staccato bursts. "Are you just going to send me to jail when I'm done doing..." He trailed off again.

Laramie sighed, then nodded. "I understand. Given the way of the world, I wouldn't trust me either, not if I was you. But, son, if you show up in good faith, we're gonna go our separate ways."

Nic scoffed. Involuntarily. "And you want to see a guy like me walk after what I did?"

The sheriff laughed, but it was a cold, mysterious thing. "I think all of this is going to stay with you until the day you die. There just won't be a paper trail."

Nic turned to look at the man. "What does that even mean?"

Laramie opened the door and started getting out. "If I could explain that, I'd probably have a better plan, but I can't, and I don't. Now, grab that box and let's go have a sit in your living room."

Nic wasn't smiling. "More story time."

Laramie grinned. "What is life but a joke told by the devil himself?"

The box was a lot heavier than it looked. Carved from a black wood with intricate etchings of odd geometries and polymorphous entities. Monsters became symbols and symbols became monsters.

This kind of box was familiar to Nic. Many pre-Gutenberg texts came in a similar case. While the etching was impressive, and in a style he'd never seen, it was ultimately *interesting*, but not much more.

"This is why you're willing to help me? In exchange for identifying this?"

Laramie and Nic sat in Nic's little living room, really more of a book depot than anything else. The fact that there were chairs to sit on was the only thing that made it other than just a place of piled books.

The rest of the house was no different.

Nic sat, holding the case. Laramie paced and smoked, stopping every now and then to examine this or that book. "So at some point you stopped with the Marxist, I-hate-America routine and started studying...*the occult*?"

Nic grimaced and looked at the old brown carpet that came with the townhouse.

Laramie squinted at a title and cleared his throat. "And all this is on the taxpayer dime, isn't it?"

Nic began to answer. Something tart, something sharp. But he stopped.

Laramie continued. "To answer your question: it's not that simple. Okay, go ahead and open that box."

"It's not that simple? You're talking about my life!"

Laramie grinned, cold. "Yeah, a life of this," he said, motioning to the mass of academic texts, "and a life where you fuck children hooked on drugs because you got busted for your little routine in Austin and had to move your operation down the road. That the life you're talking about, Nic?"

Nic's face twitched in fury and fear. He kept it shut.

Laramie held his gaze and nodded. "Now be a good boy and open the box."

Nic scoffed, furious. He snorted and snarled, but pried the lid open nonetheless. It gave off a hissing of air, of old dried dust and paper, with a rusty odor beneath.

He cautiously picked up the black leather-bound tome. Goldleaf filigree spelled out the Latin phrase: *Clavis Perfectum, or The Key to Perfection in the Room Between the Rooms.*

Nic looked up to Laramie, his anger erased. He gently placed the book back in the box and placed the lid back in place. "I need gloves to touch *anything* like this."

Laramie nodded. "It's valuable."

Nic paused, then exhaled. "I'm not qualified to appraise *anything* like this, but yeah. Extremely."

Laramie looked a bit sad and muttered, "We could use the money, but..."

He nodded, cleared his throat, then sat down next to Nic on the couch. "Take it out and open it to the first page."

Nic shook his head. "Seriously. This thing is probably one of a kind. I've never heard *anything* about this one. I need to wear gloves."

Laramie nodded, tapped another one out of the pack, and lit it. He exhaled and looked at the ceiling, as if a thousand miles away. "Just do it."

Nic stared at the man incredulously, then glanced down to the box in his lap. He took the lid back off, and ever-so-gently lifted the book out. Laramie reached over and took the box out of his lap so that Nic could set the book back down in his lap.

He glanced once more over to Laramie. "This should be in a museum, are you sure?"

Laramie took a drag but didn't make eye contact. He pulled out an old pocket tape recorder and set it on the coffee table in front of them. He pressed the button and the tape started rolling.

Nic shrugged, then looked down at the old tome. "It's probably from the 1300s. From the look of the binding, it wasn't made in a monastery. It was done by a professional shop for someone very wealthy. This would've only been affordable to the royalty."

He shook his head. "Under the title is a depiction of what looks like a dagger, probably ceremonial. The dagger has a unique blade, notched up and down the length like it's actually some sort of key. Like a literal key, not a figurative one as would be the case in much of earlier medieval alchemy. The hilt and pommel appear to be ornate, but I can't tell much more from the picture on the front."

He paused and looked at Laramie's cigarette. "You really shouldn't be smoking that with this book in the room, the smoke damages—"

Laramie shook his head. "Open it."

Nic wanted to object. *Everything* about this was wrong. *Everything* he'd gotten himself into, and *everything* that Laramie had forced him into.

His fingers grazed the black leather and touched the fraying edges of the pages.

He turned his hand and opened to the very first page, and he swore that, for the briefest moment, the letters on the yellowed parchment had rearranged themselves.

Then his telephone rang. Not his cellphone, but the landline his old-fashioned mother insisted he have.

It was startling. No one had ever called that number before. He looked at the little shelf under the end table, and yeah, there it was, ringing and blinking.

Laramie continued his thousand-mile stare into nothingness. "Answer that, right now."

Nic scrambled, holding a priceless tome in one hand and rooting for a phone he'd forgotten about with the other. His fingers searched, closed around the receiver, and brought it to his ear. "Hello?"

"Nicolas Jobim."

Nic had spoken on hundreds of garbled phone calls in his life, but had never heard anything like this. It was intelligible, and lacking identifiable background noise, but there was a crackle and whoosh he'd never heard before.

The word that came to his mind to describe the sound of the phone call was "dusty."

Old and dusty.

Ancient.

Pre-ancient.

And something of that age, of the impression of how old it sounded, took him out of his mind. It took his breath away.

Laramie slapped his knee.

Nic snapped back to where and when he was.

"Yes, this is Nicolas—"

He was interrupted by the voice. "Please open the *Clavis* to the first page and read aloud the contract."

"Okay, what?"

"Open the *Clavis* to the first page and read aloud the contract."

His mind reeled and spun in webs of impossibility.

"How the hell did you know—"

"Please. Time is of the essence. Open the *Clavis* to the first page and read aloud."

Nic continued to sputter, but his hands did not. He looked down and they had opened the book to the first page.

His sputtering ceased and his lips began to recite the words in front of him: "I, Nicolas Jobim, son of Rafael and Amadora, do willingly—"

Laramie grabbed the phone from Nicolas and hit the button to hang up.

There was a tinkling and chirping sound. Nic's cell phone in his pocket began to ring.

He looked at Laramie, baffled, frightened, and suspicious.

Laramie took a drag. "Answer that."

Nic took the phone from his pocket. The caller ID said plainly, "Unknown Caller."

Nic answered. "Hello?"

The voice returned. "Please open the text to the first page and read aloud the contract of ownership."

"What the fuck is this? How the fuck did you... Who are you? Who is this?"

Laramie nodded again. "Hang it up, and turn it off."

Nic did as he was told, but his demeanor had changed. "Sheriff, just what in the hell was that all about?"

Laramie's cell rang. He took it out of his pocket, glanced at the caller ID, and powered it off. "That would've been for you too. Now put it back in the box. Let's take a ride."

Nic rolled the window down. His state of mind couldn't accommodate Laramie's cigarette smoke. "Thought you were gonna quit, Sheriff."

Laramie tipped his ash out the window and didn't say anything.

The puzzle pieces whirled but couldn't assemble themselves into a whole.

"Okay, Laramie, how the fuck did you do it?"

"I didn't."

"Bullshit."

"Scout's honor."

Nic grinned a cynical grin. "This is some kinda scam, some kinda con. You set me up to get arrested so you could run this game on me, didn't you?"

"Nope. I saw the books in your car and knew I had the right guy. Serendipity or some such."

Nic shook his head and scoffed. "This is some kind of sick game."

Laramie nodded emphatically. "That's what I've been saying for forty-odd years now."

Nic turned and looked at him. "Why are you doing this? I don't understand what you'd have to gain by doing this unless you're just nuts."

They pulled up to a stop sign and Laramie looked around but didn't stop. "Okay, then how did I do it?"

"Getting phone numbers is easy."

They pulled into the police station parking lot, mostly empty at nine in the morning.

Laramie and Nic walked inside, Nic carrying the box. Every phone rang, one after another, as long as Nic held the box.

Laramie sat behind his desk, feet up, thousand-mile stare into a blank wall. "It's about a thirty-foot range, that's what I was able to establish. As long as you've got the book, or the box with the book in it, it's gonna do that."

Nic's hands were shaking, even though he didn't believe what was happening in the world around him.

Laramie slid the pack of smokes across the desk to him. Nic took one out, lit up, and coughed. "You've had this thing in storage since the nineties?"

He nodded. "Yeah. I took it out one time in the late nineties when we got cell phones, just to try it out. As you saw..."

"Who is the person calling?"

Laramie just shook his head.

"So, the second you open that book, you get a call from someone telling you to read a contract in the front of it saying that you own it, that's it?"

Laramie closed his eyes and rubbed them with the heel of his hand. "And that you will dutifully carry out the rituals and responsibilities enumerated."

"And did you?"

Laramie snapped back to the present. "No."

Something about Laramie's denial sounded off. "Did someone else?"

Laramie took a deep breath.

"Who?"

"My wife Janelle."

The phones in the main office continued to wail. They'd taken the one in Laramie's office off the hook, but a kind of silence had settled over the world after Laramie's words. They smoked, but didn't speak.

Laramie's last words had spoken volumes.

The cigarette finished, Nic stubbed it out in the ashtray. He stood, closed the door to Laramie's office, and sat down and looked at the floor.

"You haven't had one in a few years, I take it?"

Nic looked up at Laramie.

"A cigarette, I mean."

Nic slid the pack back over to himself. Winstons. He tapped one out and lit up.

He shook his head. "About eight years, I think."

Laramie smiled. "It's probably easier to quit when you're younger."

Nic nodded. "I guess it's the staying quit that's the tough part. You know the quitting is gonna be tough. But I guess we underestimate what life is gonna be like without them."

Laramie smiled, sadly.

"What happened, Sheriff?"

"Bartholemew Anderson! This is the Smithville police. We are coming up to the house! Come out with your hands up!"

Sheriff Grady wiped his neck with a black bandanna and hung up the handset. His three-car show of force was about halfway up the long dirt road from the highway to Nelson Garvey's bizarre mansion. They'd been here about two months before and it looked like Worm hadn't done much to keep up with the growth on the sides of the road. This made the little dirt road narrower, more claustrophobic.

Deputy Laramie leaned in the passenger side window. "Keep on, boss?"

Grady shook his head and gave a bitter little chuckle. First Worm, and now Deputy Do-Right. He glanced at Laramie, who smiled back. Both men knew there was little love between them, and both men knew that Grady didn't respect or approve of Laramie.

He had his reasons. Reasons he said out loud, and reasons he didn't.

It was the ones that he didn't say that mattered though.

He wracked his mind for words to slap the obstinate deputy, but found himself at a loss.

"You look worried, boss."

Grady peered over his reflector shades. *Fucking bold little bastard, aren't you?*

Laramie kept going. "When we saw him last month, he looked...very different."

Grady wiped his neck again. "I guess 'very different' means 'like a fucking psycho'?"

"That'd be about it, Chief."

Grady pushed his glasses back up the sweaty ridge of his nose. "I don't let every little thing scare me, Laramie. Just being cautious is all. Let's go on up to the house."

Laramie nodded and motioned to the car behind his. *We're going in.*

They drove up, and as the three cruisers got closer, the grounds of the mansion came into view. But even while approaching it was almost impossible to describe how odd this house was. From above, it would have been shaped like a five-pointed star, with each arm a different length. It made no sense; it just didn't work.

Some aspects of it were normal. Expensive imported brick, lavish gardens and fountains in front, but nothing the builders did to make this place normal worked. One could almost imagine their deliberations, trying to make sense of Nelson Garvey's bizarre demands, trying to make anything about this house functional and normal.

Apart from that, it was easy to notice that Garvey's decision to hire Worm as a groundskeeper had been a mistake as well. He was hardly the natural choice. Grady couldn't remember a day in which Worm, or any of the degenerate clan that sired him, had worked or done anything constructive. They lived in shacks on the banks of the river, no electricity, no running water.

And most people assumed that Worm's dad had been his uncle.

Now, why would a New York fancy-pants hire a worm like Worm? Unknown.

And what occasion would Garvey have to make the acquaintance of Worm in the first place? Also unknown.

Where was Nelson Garvey now? Unknown.

But all of this paled in comparison to the original question; *Why would Garvey build this monstrosity in the first place?*

Springtime in Smithville is a time of rain and overwhelming green growth, and it looked like Worm hadn't lifted a finger to beat back the foliage that reached in from every angle. At this rate, Grady estimated, no one would even know this place was here in just a few years. The road from the highway would fill with grasses, then brush, then become indistinguishable from the forest around it.

The loudspeaker spoke up and said, "Bartholemew Anderson! This is Sheriff Grady. Come on out, we need to talk to you."

The cops got out of their cruisers into the early afternoon heat, the riot of growth adding a green humidity to the air.

But their eyes were on the house and its broken geometry.

Laramie shook his head. "It's hard to even look at."

One of the other two cops, Martin Groenbeck, blinked and held them shut. "It gives me a headache. Can you imagine what a freakshow it is inside?"

The other, Gil Umberto, laughed out loud. "If you can't get me into a funhouse at the state fair, I sure as shit ain't going inside that bastard!"

They all laughed, a hint of discomfort inside their camaraderie.

"You ain't got no permission to go inside."

All four men whirled around, hands on the butts of their revolvers.

Worm stood in the path leading through the garden of statues and flowers, the carefully laid plantings going quickly back to nature. Some of the statues already had kudzu hiding faces and limbs, and the fountains were still.

He wore old, faded overalls covered in green and brown stains, and as the breeze shifted, they caught a whiff. This man didn't bathe at all, or wash his clothes. His beard and hair were a single thing, knotted and foul.

What had been simple degeneracy when they'd seen him last had become animalia.

The policemen stood tongue-tied.

"What do you want? State your business or begone."

Grady was still gaping, so Laramie spoke up. "Mr. Anderson, has Mr. Garvey returned? We'd like to speak with him."

"No."

Grady snapped to, and for a moment glared at Laramie. "Okay, Worm. Where is he? Enough with the bullshit."

Worm's expression didn't change. "He's not here."

Grady took a menacing step forward. "Where is he?"

Worm's expression stayed the same. "I have no idea. He's not here. You need to leave."

Grady took another step up. Groenbeck and Umberto did too. "Put your hands on top of your head, Worm."

Worm shrugged, expecting this. He did as he was told and got cuffed. The sat him on the trunk of Laramie's cruiser. Grady yelled at him a bit, but it didn't make Nelson Garvey reappear. He told Laramie to stay and watch Worm while he, Groenbeck, and Umberto had a look around the grounds.

Laramie had never actually spoken with Worm before by himself. He found the experience more than a little disorienting.

"Bartholemew, right? Do people call you Bart?"

"People call me Worm."

"Well, I know that, but that's not particularly nice, is it?"

Worm said nothing.

"What does your family call you?"

"They don't call me anything. They left when he called me."'

Laramie nodded, glad he was wearing his imitation Wayfarers. He knew his expression might give away his disgust, even the hint of fear that this place, and this man, elicited.

"Well, what *did* they call you?"

Worm looked at the ground. "My momma called me Thufu."

Suddenly little shivers broke out over Laramie's skin. "That's a...different kind of name. Was it like a nickname?"

Worm shook his head and grinned, a drunken thing, even though it was obvious he hadn't been drinking. "My people come and go on these rivers. Always have. And we always meet you, with your guns and your badges, acting like you know what it's all about."

Laramie nodded. "I read that. Most of the river people are east of here, in Louisiana and Mississippi. Is that what you're talking about?"

Worm didn't say anything.

"Thufu. Is that like a family name?"

"It's my church name."

Laramie was positive that neither Worm nor any of his clan had ever darkened the doorways of any of the churches in the area. He doubted they had ever done so anywhere ever.

"I've never heard of that. Where's your church?"

"Back home. That's where they went."

"Where's home?"

Worm said nothing. As far as he knew, Worm and his family had been here for several generations.

"Did you guys settle here? From Louisiana or Mississippi?"

"No."

"Then where are you guys from?"

"Every river leads to the sea, and every sea knows the land by the river. It's all water and mud. Don't you know we're all from the same dirt?"

"So I guess you guys are from all over. I can respect that."

"Liar. You couldn't respect me. Or us. That's not what it's all about."

"Oh, what is it all about?"

"Well, probably me standing here in handcuffs."

"You sold some art at the antique shops that we think you lifted from here."

Worm just looked at him. "You don't know what you're talking about."

"Is that so? I'm going to show you what they gave us, and you can tell me where you got it."

"I didn't sell anything to anyone."

Laramie walked over to the rear passenger door of his cruiser and took out a cardboard box. He set it on the trunk next to the cuffed Worm.

He took out an ornate silver playing card case. "Does this jog your memory?"

"No."

"No? That's all you've got to say?"

He didn't say anything else. No furtive eye movement, no fidgeting, nothing.

While this didn't spell out any sort of innocence, it certainly didn't help their case.

He showed Worm a small painting in a silver frame. "Apparently this one is a surrealist painter from the 30s and 40s. It's probably worth more than my house and car combined."

"No idea. Never seen it. Don't know what it is."

It was becoming clear to Laramie that Worm had been cuffed and questioned much of his life, so this may have been an exercise in futility.

He took out the weirdest thing yet, a carved wooden box, about two by two. "We weren't sure about this one. We called the university in Austin and they said don't open it, that it could break. So does this ring any bells?"

For the first time he saw something behind Worm's eyes. Fear. He hid it really well, but it was there. The odd thing was that Worm seemed to be afraid not of having stolen the box, but of the box itself. His body language cringed away from the box, like...

Laramie thought it through. There was no way they would be able to pin this on Worm.

Some places in the city have security cameras, but not antique shops in small towns out on the interstate. There was no signed receipt, nothing.

Grady probably just wanted to come out here to instigate an altercation with Worm, then arrest him for that and tack on the charges for selling stolen stuff. But Worm hadn't taken the bait, and Grady wasn't going to throw the first punch with all three deputies watching. Not with the tension between himself and Laramie.

They appraised one another, a silent understanding passing between.

He didn't have the goods on him, but something about this old wooden box freaked Worm out.

Grady, Groenbeck, and Umberto rounded the house.

Grady tilted his white hat back and looked around. He shook his head. "You ladies trade any interesting gossip?"

Laramie shook his head. "Bartholemew here is unfamiliar with the contents of this box."

Grady sighed. "Well, this was a fool's errand. Glad you got to make a new friend though."

Laramie smiled but said nothing.

No, thought Laramie. *We haven't got anything, and my boss is a stupid asshole, but this isn't something I'm going to ignore until the forest reclaims it and you can't even see the road from the highway.*

He put the box of stolen goods back in his cruiser and they left Worm to his own devices.

By the time Laramie next laid eyes on Worm, he'd be sheriff.

Janelle made spaghetti with meatballs and garlic bread. She made the meatballs herself, but the garlic bread was from Brookshire Brothers. She'd always give him an appraising look on his first bite of the spaghetti, but never with the garlic bread. She'd look away.

It was one of their millions of silly little jokes between them.

The jokes began in high school, despite the fact that his dad had been chief of police before that insufferable prick Grady. Despite the fact that Sheriff Laramie the first had put her family members away for nothing more than being the wrong color at the wrong place and wrong time. He'd been an angry, abusive man who never knew of their secret affection in his life. He'd died choking on hatred and emphysema, pushing away the hand of the son who wanted to hold his father's hand in those last moments.

He'd never seen that son's girlfriend sitting in the waiting room, quietly praying for the painless passing of a man who had inflicted his pain on others. And he'd never seen that girlfriend comforting a crying son, a recent addition to the Smithville Police Department, at his funeral.

But Grady had. And he held her against Deputy Laramie.

Didn't matter. Not to Deputy Jacob Laramie.

Jokes about garlic bread and spaghetti with the woman he loved were what mattered.

"So what's in the box, Officer?" She smiled, curious.

"Well, today we went and confronted Worm about some stolen stuff he was trying to fence at some of the antique shops. Turns out that some of it was really, really valuable and that he probably lifted it—"

She finished that thought for him. "From the mansion that rich guy built back in the woods out on Highway 95?"

"None other. But he didn't crack. There's no way to prove it, and he knew it."

She took a bite, thought about it. "So what can you do about it?"

He shrugged and let out a bitter little laugh. "Zip. Nothing. Nada. Just like what happened a few months back with him shooting that other freak."

They sat there a moment, digesting this.

"I talked to him a bit. Worm. I get that he could've been someone else if he'd been born in different circumstances."

She blew out air. "They're hard to sympathize with."

Worm and his people had always been associated with the Klan and other creepy criminality. The lowest figures on the totem pole of Smithville felt very little solidarity with one another.

He sighed. So many things didn't have solutions.

"So what's in the box?"

He stood and walked back to the living room and brought the box back to the dining room table. A small painting, a silver playing card case, and the carved wooden box.

She fingered the lid of the wooden box. "It looks like you just pry it off—"

He put a hand over hers. "Evidence. We're not supposed to open that. I think. At least I think I think. We called the antiquities department at the university and they said don't open it."

Janelle shrugged. "Shame. What if it's a winning lotto ticket from the court of Louis the 14th?"

He laughed. "If this does belong to the guy that had that mansion built, he probably already won the lotto. Jesus, you should see that place."

She shook her head. "I've heard the gossip. Weirder than weird. But if Worm is there? Yeah, no thanks."

"Oh, c'mon. He's just misunderstood. We should invite him over for some garlic bread from—"

"Don't you dare, mister!"

They laughed. Everything around them stopped except that love and that laughter. They did the dishes. They watched a three-episode tape of *The X-Files* rented at the Blockbuster where she worked in the next little town on the map.

But that box wouldn't let Jacob Laramie go.

The mysteries of Mulder and Scully couldn't stop his mind from turning back to that carved wooden box. He just imagined opening it, over and over. The thoughts never turned to the contents of the box, just that he should open the box.

Didn't matter that it was evidence that he should've returned to storage before he left work. Didn't matter that they'd been told by the experts not to open it. Didn't matter that it wasn't his.

He just wanted to open it.

So he snuck out of bed and down the hallway to the dining room. He lifted the box from the table, carried it to the living room, and sat in his recliner, turning on the little lamp on the end table.

The wood was dark, covered in confusing geometrical forms that twisted into gargoyle-dragon-kraken things. His mind flashed back to an artist that all the potheads had loved in high school. MC Escher. Yeah, that was his name.

Three-dimensional optical illusions. Yep. That's it.

He felt around the sides for seams and couldn't find any, but if he put one hand on each side and levered it up just a bit...

There was a whooshing sound, like someone had just opened a can of soda.

The lid came off and a strong dusty odor assailed his nostrils.

The smell of time itself. Time unimaginable. Time that made the age of this box seem like the blink of an eye.

There was a book inside the box. An illuminated text. One of those books with pictures of weird things in the margins.

Bound in black leather, literally sewn together. A picture of some sort of dagger/key thing, and the title: *Clavis Perfectum, or The Key to Perfection in the Room Between the Rooms.*

He opened it.

The phone rang.

There's only one reason they'd be getting a call in the middle of the night: a police emergency. But there was a wild, windy noise coming out of the receiver, and a different voice than he knew on the line.

"Please open the text to the first page and read aloud the contract of ownership."

"Hello, is this dispatch?"

"No, open the text to the first page and read aloud the contract of ownership."

"Okay, if this isn't dispatch, who is this?"

"That is immaterial. Read aloud the contract of ownership."

"Honey, who are you talking to?" Janelle's voice came from the top of the staircase.

He glanced down at the strange book in his lap. His hands moved of their own accord to open the book, and his eyes cast across the letters reassembling themselves before his very eyes.

"I, Jacob Fleming Laramie, son of—"

"Honey! What's going on? Are you going to be going into work? Is everything okay?"

The voice spoke. "Please commence reading immediately. Time is of the ess—"

Janelle's voice cut through. "Jacob? Baby?"

Her plaintive tone changed things. That wasn't dispatch on the line. This was something completely and utterly alien to him. Cold needles of sweat broke out on his back and forehead.

He exhaled hard. "It's just a wrong number, honey."

The voice on the phone calmly retorted, "This is not a wrong number. Please read aloud—"

He hung up the phone, then left it off the hook.

He called up to his wife. "It's nothing. I'm going to run this box out to the car so I don't forget it in the morning."

When he got out to his car, the voice came through the police radio.

"Please read aloud the text—"

He tossed the box in the trunk and looked up to the clear, starry sky. He listened to the world beneath his feet, spinning through a universe that made a lot less sense than it did yesterday.

Janelle snored softly next to him on the bed. He wanted to get up, go downstairs, grab that book from the trunk of his car and read that preface, provision, whatever, to the caller. He wanted to see what would happen. He wanted to know what would happen.

He wanted a fucking cigarette.

He wanted to sleep.

Just go get it.

Heck, just turn on the light in the car and read it over the CB to the guy.

The caller.

How the fuck did that guy know when someone opened that box? How was that possible?

But no matter what angle he tried, he knew he wasn't going to make that dog bark.

Because what the caller was doing wasn't possible.

It was impossible.

Worse than that.

Magic.

Something he'd never considered for more than a few seconds of concerted thought. Something that never occupied more than that amount of time in his head because it was absurd, it was stupid.

Sure, he lived out in the country and the old folks had their superstitions and their folk magic. The black folks had their version too, as did the Mexicans.

The tent revival crowd had their version as well.

Faith healing and prayer circles.

But it didn't cure anything or make poor folks any less poor.

Superstitious bullshit that didn't budge the real world in any way, shape, or form.

Hope for the hopeless at best, a con and a scam at worst.

Magic.

A weird wave of nausea hit, and he felt unmoored from his life and himself. Floating above a world where up is down and black is white and nothing is impossible. If this book and that caller were possible... What else was possible?

He felt a chill, and the hair stood up on his arms.

He wanted to go read that passage to the caller, and then he wanted to read the rest of that book. *Clavis Perfectum.*

Was the book supposed to make you perfect, or make something else perfect?

But the thoughts went soon to another place.

This thing is dangerous.

I've never heard of anything requiring a statement of ownership unless something permanent is supposed to happen. Something that requires consent.

You have to agree to take ownership of the book.

Like you have to invite a vampire in.

You have to agree with what this thing is going to do, with whatever it means by perfection.

And eventually he slept.

He tossed, he turned, and he soaked the sheets in sweat. He dreamed of limitless caverns beneath the earth, of infinite staircases under black seas and impossible labyrinths between stars. He heard whispers of words, Janelle speaking a solemn vow in her wedding dress, Worm begging something of the sky, Chief Grady screaming wordlessly. Car doors, telephones, CBs, and cigarettes crackling and glowing with each inhalation.

"Jacob, honey, the boss said he wants to see you when you get here, so go on in. I don't think he's on a call."

Mary Lee, the old blue-haired secretary, smiled and looked back to her crossword.

Great. What now?

"I'm going to go ahead and go on in..."

Grady tended to have these ambush lectures about once a month, where he would invent some dereliction in Jacob's performance, lecture him repeatedly, and make sure he left his office door wide open so everyone in the office would get to hear.

These public lectures were just one of the ways that Grady worked to force Laramie out. But Jacob wasn't about to go. Smithville was his home. His dad had been chief, and one day he would be chief.

It's who he was, what he was born to do.

But there was even more to it. His father had been a bad man, a racist cop during a racist time. They'd never talked about it before his old man died, but they both knew it was there.

Regret. Shame. Disgust.

He married Janelle just a few weeks before his dad died.

Janelle's dad died when she was a little girl, so the obvious question had been: Should Jacob's dad walk her down the aisle?

But nobody asked that question. No one asked Janelle, or Jacob, or his dad.

In the end, she walked herself down the aisle. Jacob saw, as she turned in that brief moment and flashed her million-dollar smile to the old man, that he couldn't meet her gaze, and the only tear he'd ever seen from his dad appeared for that terrible, brief moment at the corner of his eye.

Grady didn't attend.

As Jacob crossed the threshold of Grady's office, the older man looked up from the funnies in the local newspaper and the smile fell from his face, the permanent, scheming scowl when in the presence of the younger man returning in full force.

"You care to tell me why you walked off with evidence last night, boy?"

Grady had never called him "boy" before. Lots of implications with that word that Laramie wasn't okay with. But what Grady was threatening him with this time was more than mere harassment.

He was saying, none too subtly, that Laramie was a thief.

Grady knew, as did everyone else here, that Laramie was no thief.

There were no directions yesterday from Grady that he was supposed to take the box straight back to the office. Theirs was a very small department, and had never been strict about anything like that. He was in charge of this case because he'd been the one to respond to the call from the antique shop that had bought the property from Worm.

But...technically, Grady was correct.

He shouldn't have left it in his car, much less shown it to Janelle.

He should've taken it back to the office and locked it up.

He was caught flat-footed, busted.

A thin, mean smile appeared on Grady's thin, mean face.

"How the hell did you manage to forget that you're supposed to take very pricey evidence back to the office where it belongs?"

Laramie shook his head, contrite. "Boss, you're completely right. I guess it just slipped my mind thinking about how—"

He paused. He prided himself on being a model police officer, a modern police officer. Not some backward, corrupt, speed-trap cop.

Grady finished for him, "It slipped your mind, and you guessed it would slip my mind too?"

Laramie stammered, "No, absolutely not, I was just..."

A thin sheen of sweat glowed on his brow; he could feel a drop sliding down his back, between his shoulder blades.

Laramie heard the window AC unit turn on behind Grady, and listened to the sound of silence in the main of the office. All ears were tuned in to the action in Grady's office. While they all knew that Grady was a son of a bitch, they also worked for the man. He was the boss, not Jacob Laramie.

Grady was standing, looking at him. Laramie had been sideswiped by all this. He knew he was going to get it from Grady for something, but this pettiness was a new low.

He snapped back to the present. "I'll run out to my cruiser and grab it."

Grady was walking with him. They walked through the office—all conversations stopped, all eyes averted—and out the front door.

"So, boy, tell me. Did you really think you'd get away with it?"

They walked around the car to the trunk. "Chief, I made a mistake, that's all. You know I wasn't—"

Grady interrupted. "Don't tell me what I know, boy."

Jacob felt his fists tighten into steely balls. *Just one punch...*

Laramie fished the keys out of his pocket and opened the trunk.

"Like I said, Grady, I made a mistake. Sorry to get your hopes up, old man."

The cardboard box was right there in front of them, with the little painting and the silver playing card holder. But the wooden box containing the book was missing.

Grady grinned and clapped him on the shoulder. "Hope springs eternal, boy. You and I ain't done. Not by a long shot."

He put on his lights and blew right through stop signs. Tires squealed and gravel flew around corners. He slammed into his driveway and the tires skidded. He barely touched the ground as he sprinted for the front door

He figured that she'd be in the front of their house, attending to her gardening. She lived for her flowers.

Halfway to the door, he realized her red Camry hatchback wasn't in the driveway. She would've called the dispatcher, her friend Shelly from church, and she would've called him to let him know she'd been called in to work.

His feet didn't slow down, and the key was in the lock and the doorknob turned. "Janelle! Janelle, are you here!?"

Silence.

A drop of sweat slid between his shoulder blades and down his back. *She's not here.*

He picked up the phone and called Blockbuster in Bastrop where she works. She's not there and hadn't been called into work.

But he knew this.

He knew it in his gut.

His feet knew it as well as they carried him running to his car, and his hands knew the ways to turn the wheel to take him down the highway and down a long, overgrown driveway to what he knew to be true.

Worm cried because he knew what was coming, and he knew why. And he knew he'd done what he could, but the blame would still be his.

He wasn't wrong either.

The cruiser's lights were on, but no siren. The young cop overshot and slammed the brakes, barely missing the negro girl's car and ending up with half of the front end of the cruiser embedded in a privet hedge covered with kudzu.

Worm stood next to the open front door to the enormous alien mansion peering in, shaking.

The young cop, the same one from the day before with the box of stolen shit, including the book, was already on him, grabbing him and throwing him against the doorframe, screaming, "Where is she? Where is she, you fucking piece of shit?"

He was bigger, a lot bigger than this little pig, but like all little pigs, he'd gladly empty Worm's head with his pop gun. And he'd get away scot free. Because everyone knew that Worm, and anyone like Worm, only existed because the little piggies were so very generous.

But the piggies' generosity and patience with him were at an end.

The nightstick came out, stabbing into his sternum, and the air blasted out of his chest. He doubled over and the nightstick came down on the ribs in his back. He fell to the ground and the nightstick went up, then down, again and again.

Blood trickled from his mouth and his tongue traced the bloody backs of newly loosened teeth. He wasn't sure at what point that part had happened.

A kick to his side rolled him over onto his back, and he finally screamed. A long, pathetic lament. But it was cut short by the nightstick across his throat, pressed in until his mouth opened involuntarily, and a revolver shoved inside.

All that exertion has calmed the piggie a hair, and he now asked again, "Where is she?"

The piggie must've seen his attempts to speak because he removed the revolver and eased off the nightstick.

"I told her, I begged her, not to go in there!"

"If you shot her, you're a dead man, Worm. If you touched a fucking hair on her head, you're a dead man, you motherfucking piece of shit!"

The pistol slammed into the side of his face.

The front door was yet another odd detail to Nelson Garvey's alien mansion. It was just a regular external door with a couple little steps leading up to it. Not at all the grandiose thing that this house should require. More utility than anything else.

It opened into a cramped, tiny little square corridor with a door to the front, left, and right. And there was no light. Once the front door closed behind them, all light left their world.

Cramped.

Lightless.

And with the horrendous stench of Worm, airless and claustrophobic.

In his right hand was his service pistol, and his left reached for his little Maglite.

"Don't get any ideas, Worm. I will fucking kill you."

But something in Worm's breathing told Laramie that the man wasn't going to do anything. It came fast and shallow, punctuated by little sobs punctuated.

The man had begged, pleaded, that he not be forced into that house. That's what he called it. *That house.*

His eyes shifted back and forth, and Laramie sensed that he was about to bolt out into the big green woods. Laramie smiled. "Do it, Worm. Run."

He raised his pistol to let the man know exactly what would happen if he were to do what he was told.

"Now, turn around and take me to my wife."

"Wife?" His eyes were wide despite his battered and bloody face.

The gun pressed into his eye socket. "You got something to say about that, Worm?"

"Aren't you the old sheriff's boy?"

Laramie's lips pulled back into a snarl. A worm like Worm wasn't allowed to have thoughts about his marriage, his wife, or his lineage.

"Your pappy let you marry a negro girl?"

Laramie's gun was already extended, so it was just a matter of pulling the trigger. The tiny space glowed in saturated yellows and purples, and Worm's face contorted in pain. He might not regain the hearing in that ear.

Laramie hit him with the pistol again.

"Don't ever speak of them again, Worm. Those words do not belong in your mouth."

In the little light of the cramped foyer, Worm cringed against the corner, trying to simultaneously avoid Laramie and go no farther into *that house.*

Laramie reached to his left and turned the knob, moved into the opposite corner and nodded, pointing the pistol and the little Maglite into the next room.

This tiny room made little sense either, containing nothing but a phone on the wall and another door. Another cramped, windowless space.

Laramie stuck the flashlight between his teeth and pointed what he assumed was the way farther inside. Worm's eyes were wide with fright, and he stammered between bloody lips. "You don't want to go no further in there!"

Worm just gaped at him, blood trickling from the corner of his mouth, one eye swollen almost completely shut.

Laramie reached over and tried the phone. Just a regular phone with a regular dial tone. He hung it up and held the pistol and flashlight in a tactical stance. Worm smelled like moldy shit.

He gestured with his flashlight. "Where does that door go?"

Worm whispered, "Further...in there."

"No shit, asshole. Fucking march, now."

Worm just stared back, quivering. He viewed going forward only slightly more favorably than he did the gun. But Laramie had convinced him that it was one or the other.

His hand went to the knob, and he held his breath and went farther in.

A corridor, black and lightless, cramped and airless. A door at the opposite end, and doors to the right and left.

Laramie motioned left and right to the doors. "Which way did she go, Worm?"

He looked down. He whispered and pointed to the door on the right. "She had the book. She would've went that way."

Something giant, yet unspoken, passed between them at that moment.

Laramie motioned. *Move.*

"You know about that book, don't you, Worm?"

Worm walked into the little empty corridor. Unfinished sheet rock, empty light fixtures in the ceiling, but no light switches...

"Answer the question, Worm."

Worm turned to regard him. "I know the *Clavis*."

Laramie scoffed. "I had no idea you people could read."

Worm looked at him with a kind of sad awareness. "I can't read."

"Then how the fuck do you know the *Clavis*?"

He nodded. "The *Clavis* isn't for me to read. Not for my people to read."

"Are you fucking with me, Worm? Is that how you want to die?"

Again, Worm looked at him with more of the sad awareness. "That ain't what it's all about, least not for me."

"Either you're as fucking stupid as people think or—"

For a brief moment, his terror for Janelle was supplanted by a rational light.

Nothing about this fit with his understanding of the universe.

Nothing.

"It doesn't affect you if you can't read?"

Worm didn't say anything in reply.

"Open that door and keep going."

Worm gingerly grabbed the knob and stepped through.

Into another tiny, cramped, lightless corridor, this one with a door at the far end and one to the right. He stopped short, eyes rolling around in terror like a steer in a cattle chute.

He whispered, "Please don't shoot me when you...hear it."

"Hear what, Worm? I don't hear anything but your fucking breathing in this goddamn maze." He stopped, another revelation.

"Is this whole house a maze, Worm?"

"Yeah, it's a maze."

Laramie's face screwed up into a hateful rictus. "Do you know the way through or not?"

"I know the way to...where she would've went. I don't know the rest."

Laramie shook his head in frustration, fear, and hate. He screamed, "Janelle! Janelle! Where are you?!"

Worm crouched down, covered his head, and whimpered.

"Get up, you fucking—"

"Pleeeeease…"

That wasn't Worm's voice. It didn't come from Worm's mouth. It didn't come from Laramie's mouth.

It didn't come from any mouth.

It came from the fucking walls around them, and bounced around the little corridor.

Neither moved a muscle.

It came again.

"It's so dark…so empty…so hungry…"

It was a man's voice, beyond desperation, beyond terror and numbness.

Worm bolted. Laramie knocked him unconscious.

He tried to silence his breathing, for the little sounds of his heart to be smaller and less noticeable. It had made a lot of noise, belting Worm across the temple with the butt of his gun and his form collapsing in this tiny space.

It had been a pure reaction, as had everything since leaving the police station. A reaction to confusion, terror, and incomprehensibility. A reaction to all the little touchstones in life becoming alien stars in an alien constellation.

He heard footsteps, a familiar cadence of feet on floors.

Janelle.

"Janelle! Janelle! Can you hear me? Janelle?"

As if from a million miles away and from within his own ear canal, he heard.

His wife. Janelle.

Crying. Sobbing. Praying.

He screamed. Terror, loss, fury, and yet part of him knew what no other part of him could admit.

"Worm, get up." Laramie hissed the words, lest speaking out loud would make *it* happen again.

Worm lay crumpled in a corner of the cramped little space, little more than the size of two regular closets. He smelled like shit and rot. His skin was stained brown and grey, and his nails were black from root to tip.

An animal, in roughly human form.

Jacob poked him with the heel of his boot, none too gently.

He squatted down and carefully felt for the bruise on Worm's head. He'd beaten the man repeatedly today, and it would be...bad if he ended up killing him.

Finally Worm grunted and groaned, followed by Laramie poking him forcefully on the big raised bruise on his head.

Worm shouted, "Fuck you, pig!" and started to rise, forgetting his place even in this place. He settled when he felt the steel circle of the barrel pressed against his head.

"You're gonna start by calling me sir. You're gonna continue by doing everything I say, and if I'm satisfied, I swear to God you'll live. If not, I swear to God you will fucking die. Do you understand?"

Then it happened again. "Who are you? I can't see! Please! Please!"

It started to their left, then bounced to the right, farther and nearer. A scream, a woman's scream.

Janelle's scream.

Unmistakable.

It began above them, then shifted to beneath them.

Jacob screamed back, "I'm here, baby, I'm here!"

He cocked back the hammer on his revolver and shined his light down at Worm. "Get on your fucking feet, and take me to my fucking wife."

Worm's eyes were wide, terrified as any cornered animal with nowhere to go.

Laramie stepped back to give the big man some room and motioned for him to rise.

Worm carefully got to his feet, keeping his hands in sight.

He turned to the door and glanced back to Laramie. Through bloody teeth he whispered, and something about the expression on his face prevented Laramie from using his fists or his gun to answer. "Are you sure? Things'll never be the same."

Laramie whispered back, his voice still steel, but now honest, "It's way too late."

Another tiny corridor with three doors, take the one to the left.

Another with two doors, none of them going left, only to the right and directly ahead.

In a maze, the idea is that you always turn the same way, so that you can find your way back by operating in reverse. This maze wouldn't offer that option. Practically every door opened into a unique arrangement of doors. One even had a staircase leading up into the black.

At this, Worm turned and shook his head. He whispered, "I've never been up there."

Laramie asked, "What's up there?"

Worm shook his head again.

Laramie stopped. "Is my wife up there?"

Worm looked at the floor. "No."

Laramie shook his head, then nodded. "How much farther?"

Worm put his hand on the knob. "Here."

It was small for a ballroom, with ceilings too high, but at least a ballroom was something normal about this house.

The floor was white marble, with steps layered down to a sunken floor around a small raised marble dais with a heavy wooden chair atop.

The floor at the bottom of those steps was *glass*.

And seeing the thing beneath the glass completed Sheriff's Deputy Jacob Laramie's break with faith in reason.

It was some sort of titanic machine, like the inside of a watch, with millions of gears, some of them indescribably enormous, heading as a column down into the earth, into the dark, where he could see no more.

On the dais, the heavy wooden chair faced a brass pedestal connected to the machine below.

In front of the chair, the *Clavis* lay splayed open.

Next to Janelle's purse and car keys.

He reached out a hand, and his wife's cries of despair emanated and echoed throughout the house. The air caught in Jacob's chest. He wanted to scream, he wanted to cry, he wanted to pray, but the God he knew didn't seem to have anything to do with the universe as it truly was: *a beast with his mind in its jaws*.

Scared. Nic had been scared before, but he stumbled over the feelings that painted his fear a deep bloody red. His life had been, by turns, relatively safe and easy. While no human knows perfect safety and ease, there are lanes we avoid because they contain death and despair, and he hadn't truly driven down any of those lanes.

Yes, his choices, his untamed character defects, had driven him to Cleo's house, and those same character defects blinded him to her plight, but none of those character defects should have driven him *here*.

Here was a different place and a different state of mind than he had bargained for. The Devil he knew had taken a wrong turn and come back as a black swan: impossible, unknowable, maddening.

The studies he had dedicated himself to, the research of medieval grimoires and the occult had never promised anything like this. They promised gnosis, a deeper understanding that would, or at least should, bring about a kind of existential fulfillment.

Or they were just chicanery.

But this wasn't, and now he truly did *know*, and wished he didn't.

He shook his head. "Jacob..."

"Sheriff. That's my name to you..." He thought about it with a tiny shake of the head. "Just call me Laramie."

Nic understood. They were going to work together on this, but Laramie was the boss. A mad, inappropriate giggle escaped his lips. He was okay with that.

Whatever they were going to do, he had no fucking desire to be the boss of it.

He exhaled, hard. "Laramie... Who else knows about this?"

The sheriff shook his head. "That I know of: you, me, and Worm."

Nic sat with that for a moment. His brows furrowed. "No one here in town knows? How is that possible?"

Laramie nodded and looked at the floor. "I made sure."

"How does that work, Sheriff?"

"By being exactly the kind of man that I hate. I made sure every scrap of paper about this vanished. And I've kept it up over the years."

A weird chill crept up his spine. "Laramie, what does 'that I know of' mean?"

Laramie took a sharp inhalation and took a file out from under his desk.

"The medical examiners through the years... After they do their part, the file gets submitted to me for approval. I always swapped the photos after they'd done their part."

He looked down at the floor again and shook his head. "Every one of them was a good person, but I made sure they lost their job and had to move on after...one of *these*."

A series of photos taken through the years: bodies on the slab, all killed by a single rifle shot through the chest, but it was the other injuries that were most distressing.

They were missing ears, noses, lips, skin scarred and burned, until these men and one woman were barely identifiable as humans, as persons.

Genitals, breasts hacked away.

And all these injuries, apart from the rifle shot, appeared to have been inflicted during years of unbelievable torment. Even in death, their expressions spoke of an unfathomable, unimaginable *knowing*.

"All of them had missing persons reports filed years, or even decades, prior. All of them had done time in the looney bin. But they vanished off the radar for years before showing up on my slab."

Nic stared at the photos but lacked the words to express the revulsion in his mind.

Laramie nodded. "And to answer that question you aren't asking: Yeah, those injuries were self-inflicted."

"So somebody out there knows about this place, this mansion...haunted house... whatever that place is, and sent *these* people?"

Laramie was expressionless. His voice barely a whisper. "I think they sent themselves. I think they were...*drawn* to it."

At this, Nic's cold sweat became colder still. "You said the guy that built the place, he vanished... How do you know he wasn't the one that sent them?"

"Because he's dead. Or...something like it."

Exasperation at accumulated impossibility crept through Nic's tone. "And how would you know that?"

"Because he's in there."

"In where, Laramie? This is crazy."

"He's in the house, and so is Janelle."

Nic's expression went flat again, and the enormity pressed in.

Laramie cleared his throat. "I know he's in there because...he's one of the ghosts in there, in the Room Between the Rooms."

"The fuck is 'the Room Between the Rooms'?"

Laramie shook his head and cursed beneath his breath. He raised his head and gave Nic a look of fear, frustration, and desperation. He ran his hand across his forehead, and Nic saw a pronounced tremble.

He'd been carrying this burden almost as long as Nic had been alive.

Nic was terrified as well; terrified that he may lose everything he'd ever worked for, and all over the same weakness that had almost cost him everything not long ago.

He looked at his own hands. The cigarettes had helped, but his hands were shaking. In the big empty office behind them (it was Sunday morning), the phones still rang in perpetuity.

"Is the guy on the phone Nelson Garvey?"

Laramie looked up from his fugue, a startled impression in his eyes. *This kid is smarter than the average Austin Pervert.*

Laramie shook his head. "I dunno. Maybe. Maybe not. I'm not sure it matters who that voice on the phone is."

Nic stubbed out his latest smoke. He'd smoked three in quick succession and his stomach was beginning to take notice. A hint of queasiness moved across the surface of his mind.

In a quick moment, he saw Laramie not as a dirty cop blackmailing him, but as a desperate man trying to... What? *Save his wife?*

Nic looked back to the files in front of him, photos of horrid disfigurement, eyes of blank madness, and a single gunshot to the chest.

"What am I looking at, Worm? And you need to tell me where Nelson Garvey is right now."

"Or you'll kill me?"

"Damn straight."

"You'll find your way out, but it'll take a day or four. That's how long it took me to get it right. And there's more than one way to get it right, but not near as many as to get it wrong."

Laramie nodded. "It sounds like it would be good for both us then."

An understanding gained, Laramie nodded toward the glass floor and the enormity beneath. "Where is Nelson Garvey, and what the fuck is this place?"

Worm grinned, a hideous visage in bloody rot. "How dark you think it'll be if you turn off your flashlight?"

Worm's eye glittered as the grin crawled across his face.

Terror and ecstasy.

"I imagine it'd be pretty fucking dark, Worm. Get to the fucking point."

"There are no points in here, Sheriff. They got lost in that maze, in those black places between doors."

"My wife, asshole, start making fucking sense."

Worm pointed to the largest wall of the room. A simple, unadorned slate of white marble.

"It's real dark at the center of the maze. Dark enough. So dark you can disappear into there. Then you go in there."

"That's a wall, you fucking birth defect."

"Not when it's dark enough it ain't."

He felt his fingers tighten on the grip of his pistol, and his eyes shifted to his wife's open purse sitting next to that goddamn book.

He walked to the bottom step before the glass floor.

"Okay, Worm, how thick is this glass? Am I gonna fall through?"

Worm shook his head and walked down the three stairs to stand on the glass floor. "It's thick. Real heavy. Nelson had to bring in cranes special just to put it in place."

Laramie walked across to the raised dais, looking down through the glass at the enormous impossibility beneath him.

"How did he keep this secret? I mean, I heard this place was really weird, but..."

Worm nodded. "All the workers who saw the inside of the house were illegals he had brought in special. I'm the only local who's seen the inside of this place."

Jacob reached down to pick up Janelle's purse, looking at the mundane things inside. Hairspray, wallet, car keys, lipstick. All the markers of normalcy inside this labyrinth of the unnatural.

He gritted his teeth. "Where is she, Worm?"

He pulled out the big revolver and tapped it against his pants leg.

Worm's indecipherable mirth evaporated, and his eyes rested on the gun.

His breathing increased. "You'll shoot me because you don't believe me."

Laramie nodded. "Yep. Where's my wife?"

Worm's hands shook and his breathing hitched in his chest. "I swear to all the gods, whichever you want, I didn't do nothing to her."

Laramie glared. "Is she lost in this maze?"

He shook his head; short, rapid, scared. "No, I swear, I told you. She's in the Room Between the Rooms." Tears filled his eyes. "I begged her. I knew I knew her. Real pretty negro girl, came from a mean family, but wasn't like them at all. Not mean to people like me." He paused, and Laramie glared. "I thought since she was nice that she'd listen, but I knew once I saw her eyes..."

"You knew what, Worm?"

"She read the *Clavis*, she didn't have no choice, and she weren't gonna stop."

He just looked at the ground, more tears falling down his grimy, bloody face, vanishing into the tangle of filthy facial hair.

He continued, "She read the words and the Throne of Knowing took her to the Room Between the Rooms."

"I don't believe you, Worm. You've got seconds, not minutes, before I put you down."

Worm's face cracked and creased. "You sit in the chair and you say the words! That's all! Once you read even the first page, it owns you. You can't stop until you sit in that chair!"

"And then what? Then what?"

"You can't stop yourself. You sit in the chair and you say the words, and when the light comes on you aren't here anymore. You're there now."

He pointed to the simple wall faced by the chair on the dais. The odd cylinder protruding from the floor of the dais, a brassy metallic thing with a slot in the top, grooved as if for an enormous key.

Laramie stood on the dais and picked up the *Clavis*.

"So if I read this book, and sit in that chair in the dark, and say the magic words, I'll end up on the other side of that wall?"

"Please don't, you won't come back."

"What's on the other side of that wall, Worm?"

"Right now, it's just the outside. Trees."

"Right now? What does that mean?"

"Nelson wouldn't listen neither, he... he can't come back, neither can she, neither can...whoever else is in there..."

"I'm gonna come back here with a bulldozer, Worm, and I'm going to break open that wall."

"And she'll be gone forever if you do..."

Laramie paused in a sharp inhalation of breath. "What do I gotta do? One more riddle out of you and you're a fucking dead man."

Worm nodded, knowing his place in the world. He looked down. Then he pointed to the brass cylinder with the grooved slot. "You need the *Clavis*, the actual *Clavis*, the Key of Perfection."

"Did you shoot him?" Nic looked alarmed.

Laramie shook his head quietly. They'd left the office and he could hear the phones stop ringing as he walked out the back door.

"No, I didn't."

A sudden chill of revulsion crept up Nic's spine. "He's not... Worm's...not still out there?"

Laramie nodded. "Yep."

Nic put out a hand and Laramie slid him a smoke. "He's been out at that mansion for thirty years, and you kept it a secret..."

"Best I could. The road up to the house from the highway grew over in just a few years. There was a back way, an old logging path. I bought that property it was on, and I keep a trail open. Sometimes I go up there..."

He trailed off, staring at the ground in front of him, the ash growing long and absurd at the end of his cigarette.

"You go up there and what, Sheriff?"

"I put my ear up to the wall and listen to the echoes of the ghost of my wife."

An expression of unknown horror crossed Nic's face, replaced by the faint understanding of Laramie's loss. His unfathomable burden. "You can still...hear her?"

Laramie nodded, eyes fixed on the gravel of the little empty parking lot.

Nic smoked, and Laramie smoked, and neither said anything. In the distance, a chorus of crickets added their sound to the eternal blue Texas sky.

Laramie flicked his cigarette to the ground and exhaled the last of the smoke from his lungs. "I suppose it's time we talk about the last time we got a call from Worm."

Nic turned to the older man, with something like respect in his eyes. "Another one of the...guys who cut off their faces?"

Laramie nodded, but something besides cigarette smoke lingered in the air.

Nic asked, "But this time was different somehow?"

Laramie stared out, either lost in thought or at a loss for words.

Nic filled in the blanks. "Different enough to make the kind of arrangement we've got."

The sheriff shook his head slightly. He hadn't chosen this life, it had chosen him, and he'd done things he wasn't proud of.

It wasn't Saturday anymore. Somehow it was Sunday. Jacob looked at himself in the rearview mirror, barely able to identify the man looking back. His ordinarily tanned skin was pasty and glistening with the sweat of terror. His eyes ringed with black fear. Uniform pasted to his skin, sweat stains down his back and sides. He smelled of rancid panic and gunpowder, knuckles scabbed.

But worst was the ripe, rank stink of having been in the presence of Worm.

Janelle's purse and the *Clavis* sat in the car seat next to him. It was only the sound of the bones in his wrist popping that broke his trance and caused him to release his death grip on the steering wheel.

That, and the sharp rapping on the passenger side window.

He was in the parking lot behind the station.

Grady was grinning like a pervert. He knocked again, then opened the door and reached in for the dark wooden box that held the *Clavis*, his eyes stopping on Janelle's purse.

His sick grin etched up a notch. "So it wasn't you that stole it. It was your wife, wasn't it? Those people just can't not steal, can they?"

That's when things went sideways.

Laramie's right hand acted before any kind of sense could travel from his head to his hand. His four fingers found the back of the older man's neck, his thumb the older man's Adam's apple, and his tricep flexed, pulling Grady bodily into the front seat next to him.

Prone. Vulnerable.

Grady twirled around to face upward while pulling his revolver as fast as a cottonmouth strikes.

He opened his mouth to scream for help, but his mouth was filled by the long barrel of Laramie's revolver, while Laramie's left intercepted the hammer coming down in a blinding flash of pain into the soft flesh between thumb and forefinger.

Laramie pressed down, the barrel stabbing the back of the man's throat in a horrible gagging of forced fellatio. Their eyes met, and Grady's protestations died as Jacob cocked the hammer and stared down at him impassively.

As far as Mexican standoffs go, this instance was decidedly one-sided.

Laramie glanced up and around at the empty parking lot.

Things were slow at the police department on Sundays in Smithville.

"I needed to see what happened when I showed you the book, the *Clavis*, before... Well, I guess before..."

Laramie trailed off, lost in thought midsentence.

It was now Monday, about forty-eight hours after he'd turned Nic's life upside down, or after Nic had turned his own life upside down, depending upon which perspective one was inclined to take.

They sat in the cluttered book depository that Nic thought of as a living room in his little townhouse.

"Before you show me what's behind door number three." Nic finished his thought for him.

Jacob nodded. "That's about that long and short of it, and...and I wish I didn't have to, son. Despite what you did. Despite who you are. No one deserves this."

Nic didn't pay any attention to that last part, as his eyes were fixed on the oblong bundle of cloth strapped with electrical tape on the little coffee table before them.

Next to the carved wooden box containing the *Clavis Perfectum*.

Nothing of its shape gave any hint to what lay inside.

Laramie leaned back in the couch and looked around the room. "Apart from the Marxist word salad you've got going here, what is the rest of all this? What is it about?"

Nic snapped back to the room, Jacob's prescient question hinting at larger things. He cleared his throat, thinking before his next words. "I suppose, in a nutshell, it's about truths that lay outside the mundane, the a deeper meaning underlying the material world."

He thought about it and nodded at his summation.

Jacob pulled out the pack and offered one. Nic nodded. Cigarettes were the silver lining to his new world.

"So it's about gnosis, I take it?"

Nic looked to the older man, a bit surprised.

A rue smile cracked the older man's face. "The old man's not so terribly misanthropic after all."

Something like a smile cracked Nic's face too, for the first time in about forty-eight hours.

Laramie continued. "I studied what I could through the years, but most of it made no sense, and never talked about the real things I'd actually seen."

Nic nodded. "Most of it is bullshit. Some of it is an honest attempt to get at the truth, however misguided, primitive, whatever."

"I guess people don't expect the truth to be fucking awful."

The smile dropped from Nic's face. "I guess not."

Laramie reached to the table and grasped the cloth bundle, taking the buck knife from his belt and cutting the electrical tape binding it. He unrolled it and Nic gasped in recognition.

Jacob sighed and nodded. "That book ain't about knowing the secrets of the universe. It's a fucking *manual*."

Nic stared, utterly and completely locked in.

"Breathe, son. You ain't done here."

Nic exhaled, hard, as Laramie handed it over to him.

It was the key that the *Clavis Perfectum, the Key to Perfection,* displayed on its front cover.

Nic stammered, "How... When did..."

Laramie let the younger man twist for a moment before letting him know. "Worm called us not too long ago. That phone line to

Nelson Garvey's mansion still works. He bagged another trespasser, but this time I went by myself. He called for me and me alone. And we burnt that fucking body."

Nic's head jerked back and forth between the impossibility in his hands, and the old man telling him its story. "Was it...like those other ones?"

Laramie shook his head slowly, back and forth. "No. Yes. All the self-inflicted injuries were there, but they'd healed. Only what grew back wasn't right."

His eyes were distant, vacant and traumatized.

"What does that mean, Sheriff?"

"Worm said it best. He said it *smelled of the deep places*"

"I don't know what that means either, Laramie."

"It wasn't normal skin, it was like a snail or a slug or..."

"A mollusk?"

"Yeah. We burned it, son. But it was still talking, up until we lit that thing up with gasoline."

"What did it say?"

"We burned it with old tires, so not even a scrap of that thing remained. Not here. Not in Smithville. Not on this goddamn planet."

"What did it say, Laramie?"

Laramie's cigarette was done. He lit another and nodded silently to himself, rocking back and forth, ever so slightly.

"It said, 'You alone among the stars, you alone in the deep and dark.' He, it, whatever it was, whatever it had been, it just kept repeating that. Fucking squirming."

Laramie put a hand over his mouth like he was going to gag. He breathed, in and out, hard. "Before I got there, Worm hacked its arms and legs off, but it kept flopping, writhing... talking."

Nic's eyes went wider. "And it had this with him?"

Laramie shook his head. "No. His...*its* car was parked on the side of the highway. So normal looking. A fucking Toyota. There was a motel key for one of the little roadside spots up the interstate. They never saw his face because it was covered in bandages. They assumed he was a burn victim. It was in the room inside a suitcase. I guess he was scouting the place out before—"

He paused again.

Nic whispered, "Before what?"

Jacob didn't answer, he just looked back with a sick fear and shook his head. "What do you see when you look at this thing, Nic?"

Nic looked back down. "It's like a gigantic key, crossed with a dagger. I don't know what this metal is though."

The blade, notched and incised up and down, was a gleaming black metal, the pommel some kind of grey stone, or bone, worn down and cracked in places. Shapes had been carved into it of snakelike coils, but little more could be discerned.

Jacob stared straight forward now, making no eye contact, lost in memory. "I took it to your alma mater in Austin, to the carbon dating lab, and I bribed the technician. All I learned was that the metal isn't on the periodic table, and that pommel...that pommel is... The term he used was 'deep time.' It's human bone, but older than the dinosaurs."

"Jacob, that's not fucking possible!"

"I grabbed it and got out of there. The whole time the technician was yelling at me, screaming at me to stop, that this was the most important discovery since...I don't know. He followed me into a bathroom, and I knocked him out and left him there."

Laramie took a breath and continued, "When I got home, I looked up what *deep time* is, and I thought about the thing underneath Dent's mansion, that machine extending down into the darkness, and the Room Between the Rooms where Janelle—"

Nic put his hand on Jacob's shoulder. "What, Laramie?"

Laramie looked back, tears in his eyes. "She's still in there, like an echo. Somehow still echoing. I'm just a man, Nic. Just a man."

Nobody saw what happened in the parking lot. Laramie spun the tires, kicking up a cloud of white limestone dust to obscure what he did to the older man after knocking him unconscious with a wicked downstroke of his revolver. No one saw Grady painfully jammed onto the passenger side floor in an obscene assembly of handcuffs. The human body wasn't supposed to be contorted like that. No one would survive long squashed in there like that.

He opened the passenger side door, grabbed a handful of hair, and pulled, but it all just came loose to a ripping and screaming.

"He's wedged in there too tight, Worm. Could you remove the sheriff from the cruiser for me?"

Jacob didn't like the look on Worm's face, but the same smile creased his own. Sadistic, hateful.

But he did appreciate how far Worm managed to throw the man from the cruiser in the process of getting him out, and that Worm had chosen a rose bush as the place where Grady would land.

There were less-bloody ways Worm could've used to get Grady out of the rose bush as well, but Laramie's mind was elsewhere. Janelle loved roses. When he got her out...

I'm going to figure it out, Janelle, and I'm going to get you out of there.

He reached into the passenger side, glanced at her purse, and closed his eyes, thinking of her face, her smile. Then his hand went to the carved wooden box next to it.

Grady wheezed and sobbed in pain on the ground at Worm's feet, chained and contorted.

Laramie squatted down in front of the bound man, holding the key to the assembly of handcuffs twisting the man into the impossible shape before him so that Grady could see.

He inserted the key, releasing the cuffs holding the other cuffs in place around his ankles, hands, and neck. Grady snapped backward against the passenger side door like a rubber band, with an awful sound of popping cartilage and bone.

And a short scream of agony.

"That's what they did to folks like me back when your daddy was sheriff."

Laramie looked up at Worm, and some of the smile faded from his face.

He squeezed his eyes shut again, as his mind flashed to the idea of Janelle knowing he'd ever done this to another human being, no matter how despicable.

He shook his head, and the cold steel returned to his eyes.

"Worm, help our new associate sit upright."

Jacob opened the ornate wooden box, the scent of impossible age on the air. He opened the book to the first page, then grabbed Grady by the hair and yanked him upright to see it as the corrupt old cop's eyes settled on the ancient page in front of him.

Something in the old sheriff's eyes changed. All the fear and fury evaporated, replaced by a blank awe.

The CB squawked out a jagged wall of hissing feedback, and Jacob reached into the cruiser to retrieve it and hold it up to the old man's face. Jacob hit the squelch button and held it.

"Say hello, Grady."

Grady looked up, all the anger and pain gone from his expression, replaced by the apotheosis of confusion. "What? What do you mean?"

The voice came from the CB. "Grady Ellis."

"What? Yes... Is..."

The voice commanded, "Read the contract of ownership on the first page of the *Clavis*."

Grady's eyes shifted to the text and his face further slackened. "I, Grady Marshall Ellis, will take ownership of the *Clavis*, and will faithfully pursue the rites and duties as enumerated within. I shall let no man obstruct me from this task. I give myself to this duty that the world be perfected..."

He trailed off, eyes blank. He stared off into the middle distance, then his head snapped to the house and a groan of unfathomable ecstasy fell from his mouth along with a long bloody rope of drool. He whispered, "You alone among the stars, you alone in the deep and dark..."

Grady looked to Jacob, all recognition of the fact of his torture absent in his gaze. "Release me."

Nic cleared his throat but didn't turn his head. He'd known Laramie was a hard cold man, but it hadn't occurred to him that he was also a mad man. They drove in Laramie's old cruiser. All the deputies had new ones, but the chief still drove this old relic. Cigarette and coffee, time and dirt.

Obsession and brokenness.

Route 95 settled into the brilliant sun and everything was golden-wreathed, brilliant green, and dusty windshield haze.

Nic asked, or stated. "You killed him."

Laramie nodded."Something like that. Yes. Maybe."

Nic filled in the blanks."He was a piece of shit."

Jacob shook his head. "Is that all you think about people?"

Nic thought for a moment, not expecting this...but then again, he hadn't expected any of this. He looked straight forward into the sun, thinking of all the things he'd gotten wrong about the world.

He cleared his throat. "I hope not."

Laramie slid a cigarette out of the pack, Winstons, and then proffered the pack to Nic. "Put all that shit out of your head, kid, because you're not any better than him, or you wouldn't be here."

Laramie sighed. "I was a good man, I really was. On the side of the angels and all that. Lot of good it did me, and I haven't been one since. Good men die in car crashes, and barn fires, of brain cancer and crib death. Nah, we're not good men, Nic, and the world needs a busload of choir boys like it needs a hole in the head."

Nic thought about this and everything else he'd failed to understand as they turned down Zapalac Road. Just a two-lane cut through a dense stand of loblolly pine. Down about a half mile, then a turn onto a dirt road to an unassuming double-wide.

"In case you didn't know, we've been driving past the Nelson Garvey property the second we turned down Zapalac here on the right. The entrance was on 95, but it's grown over."

"People forgot about this place."

Laramie shook his head, then nodded. "Best thing that could happen to them."

He sat in the driver's seat, not moving. Nic broke his fugue. "How badly am I going to regret going forward here, Jacob?"

They pulled into a dirt driveway leading to a modest shiplap-sided bungalow beneath a canopy of giant oaks and tall slender pines. He pulled around the back to an old metal garage with an older Ford pickup parked within.

Laramie blew smoke, and his eyes shifted around the sun-dappled woods outside the cruiser. "Am I Jacob to you now? I thought I was Laramie."

There was a narrow cut through the forest leading in the direction of what would be the rear of the Nelson Garvey property. Little more than a deer path.

Nic's hand went to the door handle and paused. "I know less than I did before you crash-landed in my life, because I'm fairly certain I never knew a good goddamn in the first place. What difference does it make if I call you by your name?"

They got out of the car to two thumps of old doors. Birds fluttered in the trees, and nothing more. "Doesn't matter. Not anymore."

"Do you know who I am, Grady?"

Grady remained cuffed, but not cruelly hog-tied. He stared straight ahead, but snapped to at the mention of his name. "Course I know who you are, you darkie-loving piece of shit."

He shook his head. "If your father could see you now. It's better he passed."

Red, blind fury.

Grady grinned at him, bloody gums and teeth.

Laramie wanted to knock them in, to tear them out with pliers.

He regained control.

This wasn't about Grady, this was about Janelle.

"Worm, do the people in the Room Between the Rooms see each other?"

Worm groaned and held his head, but not from the savagery that Laramie had inflicted upon him just a day before. He squeezed his eyes shut. "Every soul in there is alone." He began whimpering. "Please don't, not even this one."

Jacob turned back to Grady. "What are you gonna do when I take off those cuffs?"

Grady looked back as if Laramie had asked the single stupidest question a human ever could. He'd always assumed that tone with him, but it had all been a means of intimidation, of belittling, of ostracizing. Now it was genuine.

"I'm going to do God's work."

"What does that mean, Grady?"

If it was possible for a more confounded and perplexed expression to mar a man's face, no one had ever seen it.

"I'm going to fulfill my role as a human being, you fucking moron."

"And how are you going to do that?"

"By perfecting this world. How do you not know this? How do you not know what that book is? You were always a disappointment, but it's hard to understand how you don't understand."

"You only read the first page, Grady, if that."

"All that book does is show you what you forgot. What this inbred retard forgot," he said, motioning to Worm. Then he looked at Jacob. "What every single human being that ever has been since the Flood has—" He paused, suddenly unsure.

But it passed, quickly.

"I'll know more when I attain the Throne of Knowing. Yep, that's it. The *Clavis* is the..." He drifted, searching for words. "It's the key."

"What is the Throne of Knowing, Grady?"

Grady looked around angrily and down at the cuffs binding his hands, then down at the cuffs around his ankles. "Let me out of these right now, fucker."

"Answer the question, Grady."

Grady spat. "I don't fucking know, asshole, but I'm not a goddamn idiot who can't figure it out, unlike you!"

"Okay, what do you know about the Throne of Knowing?"

Wide-eyed, exasperated, at the end of his patience, he screamed, "I know it's right in there, and that's all I fucking need to know, now let me out of these goddamn cuffs!"

"And if I don't?"

Grady was red-faced, beginning to hyperventilate, tears flowing. "I'll fucking die! I'll fucking die and every stupid pointless breath of every stupid fucking moment of every stupid fucking life on this stupid fucking cattle-chute fucking planet won't mean a fucking thing!"

Spit, foam, and tears. "Now let me out!"

Behold. It came to Nic that he'd used that word before in life, seen it written down, and heard it from the mouths of others, but he'd never actually done it.

To behold. He beheld.

All of that. Never had done if before.

He'd put his face up to the glass at the zoo, face to face with a tiger, eyes inches apart, and his heart had gone pitter-pat.

He'd looked down at his dead father in his casket.

He had seen a car burst into flames on the side of the road while a young mother struggled with the straps of the baby seat.

He'd seen the Hope Diamond, and the radiant blue eyes of nubile freshmen girls in mid-orgasm beneath him.

He'd seen a boy jump from a twenty-story building to the concrete below.

But never once did he *behold*.

Not until now, as they stepped into a clearing that had been a sumptuous garden of statues and fountains, now taken by decades of kudzu and brush, when the shape of a man emerged from the green.

The man was tall, and large, and green. Upon closer viewing, he was naked, skin indistinguishable from mossy bark, hair matted, hanging with growing things. A dirt elemental.

Worm.

Only his eyes gave truth to the lie that he was not part of the wild flora.

Fauna, a faun, if any human could be.

And when he spoke, it was a croaking. "The ghosts grow restless, and the wind carries worry. Why have you brought this one, after so many seasons?"

Laramie did what he always did. He lit a cigarette. Worm shrank backward. "I thought... He might be the one who could help me. That maybe he could at least see the outlines of the picture."

"Is he a seeker?"

"Not like the ones we've dealt with."

"Then what is he?"

Nic felt Worm's eyes upon him, like a statue exhumed from a thousand years to pass judgement.

"He's not crazy, he's not...perverse, like those others. I think he's up to the task."

"He didn't read the *Clavis*."

"No, but he understands what it can do, what it has done. What it did."

"Does he know what has come before? What has befallen you and me?"

"He does."

"Does he understand that there is no going back?"

Nic felt the pack on his back, the oblong wooden box, and what lay within. He felt the weight of the thing it described, the Key of Perfection.

Laramie looked to Nic, and Nic looked around the clearing at gardens devoured by forest, an exotically shaped mansion hidden beneath and behind kudzu and forest.

Behold, beheld.

Worm cried, knowing he was powerless to stop a man possessed. A man driven. Much less two of them.

Jacob paced back and forth, sweaty, wild-eyed.

He'd been at it for about two hours under the blazing Texas sun.

Grady sat cross-legged, cuffed, in the shade of the cruiser, the *Clavis Perfectum* open in his lap.

Jacob looked carefully, cautiously from oblique angles at the thing happening before them. Grady was progressing quickly, impossibly fast through the thick tome, but never seemed to turn any pages.

He absorbed it, or it absorbed him

Though Worm couldn't read, and Jacob only looked from the corner of his eyes, all humans know instinctually when they witness the unnatural and the abhorrent.

Nothing changed in Grady's outward appearance, but his countenance, his expression, the very look in his eyes became steadily more wretched, alien, inhuman, and unholy by the moment.

His eyes spoke of a knowledge impossible, aeons of silence and shadow, broken only by torment. No redemption, no rescue, no such vain thing as hope. Only death incarnate.

Laramie's eyes grew blacker in time with the man before him, not for himself, or Worm, or his prisoner, or this avalanche of impossibilities that had taken him, but for Janelle.

What had she seen in these pages?

She hadn't had an easy life, but she was an innocent by choice. She had chosen to be decent and kind despite what the world had thrown at her. She'd chosen him, despite the badge, despite his father's badge and what that meant for people like her in this stretch of dirt that was her life.

Had she seen Hell? Was that what this was? Was this the Devil?

Laramie's heart went cold, with an unshakeable doubt that something as knowable as the Devil was at work here.

No, this was no Devil, no Hell, no opposite of God in his remote Heaven, no fallen angel of a rational universe.

This was none of that.

"It's time now, boy."

Laramie stopped pacing.

Grady sat calmly, steadily, the *Clavis Perfectum* closed in his lap.

Worm cried, "You can turn back! You can! We can just shoot him and bury him. Your girl is gone. Gone! *You* aren't."

Laramie wheeled, the gun in his hand pressed against Worm's temple. Worm's eyes were full of everything a steer knows in the cattle chute before the bolt penetrates the skull.

Worm's terror was clear.

Laramie's intent was clear.

He dropped the gun to his side.

"There's no going back, Worm. I have to know. I have to understand, even if there's no such thing anymore."

Worm nodded, sobbed once more, and nodded again. The die was cast.

"I was supposed to guard this place. To keep out intruders. To guide those people who sought this thing. I broke my oath, I betrayed everything I knew. Everything that my people were. But the darkness is hungry, and I can't stop it any more than I could stop you."

Grady's voice cut through. "You should shoot him, Laramie. There are worlds in every breath. He knew that. He's a traitor to fulfillment and perfection."

Calm, matter of fact.

Laramie shook his head, lowered himself to Grady's level, and unlocked the cuffs around his ankles. He left the one binding the older man's wrists.

He looked from Grady to Worm. "Do either of you doubt that I will put a bullet in you without a second of hesitation?"

Grady stared back with ancient eyes, and Worm looked back with the eyes of infinite grief. None of them blinked.

Laramie nodded. "Then we have an understanding."

He flung the cuffs that had been on Grady's ankles over to Worm.

"Put those on, Worm, we're going in."

No estimation of grief, of regret and betrayal, nor works of poetry and pain could explain the lamentation of ghosts. There are simply no words to describe their words.

"Jacob, please, please, please..."

Words reverbated and echoed around the inside and outside, from the left and right, above and below the tiny spaces inside this maze. They began two doors in, where, if not for their flashlights, they may as well have been in that place before Creation, before light itself.

"Can you hear me? Is there anybody there? I can't see where I am! I don't know where I am!"

The first voice was Janelle's. That much was obvious from the hitch in Laramie's breath, and Worm's as well.

The second was a man, a slight East Coast accent. "Hello! Somebody? Help me!"

At the first voice in these airless confines, Nic had panicked, fumbling for the door behind him, a pathetic cry of existential terror, hyperventilation, and the humiliation of shitting his pants. Not much, but enough.

Only the stench of Worm had prevented the others from knowing.

Laramie had told him of the animal fear inside the walls, and he'd duly noted those words. But they had been eclipsed by the outre experience of opening the *Clavis Perfectum*, and of Laramie's unfathomable tale.

And now here he was, in the mouth of ghosts, in true Darkness, the only place to give voice to their pain.

He was not afraid of these ghosts.

They themselves could not harm him.

But their words could.

Their confusion, their despair, their fear was not of something that could be done to them, of teeth and claws they might yet face.

No, their fear was of the moment they lived in.

Alone, in the dark, forever.

No comfort, no love, no companionship, but the memories of what they'd lost to be here, in this place.

This terrible place that existed for seemingly no reason beyond the cruelty of its purpose, which was nothing more than the infliction of cruelty.

More voices came, seemingly from farther away, a static of multitudes whispering, begging, crying for release.

And he knew.

This wasn't a mansion built by a madman.

This was a machine.

Laramie grabbed him and twisted his arm behind his back. "Kid, this is real, as real as it gets. And there's no going back! You wanted *gnosis*? You wanted to know? Now you do."

Nic gasped for air, not from Laramie's restraint, but from the truth of this place. "Just fucking charge me, Laramie! I ain't going one step farther inside this fucker!"

Jacob squeezed in. "Boy, you can, and you will. You hear them the same as me. The same as Worm. We can fix this. We can make this right."

A chill seized him as a new kind of terror turned his mind inside out.

His muscles spasmed. He screamed, high and girlish. "You're going to put me in there with them! You're going to trade me for her!"

Laramie released him and he slid to the floor. Nic started sobbing, and Jacob put a hand over his mouth. "I swear to God that isn't what we're here for. That isn't going to happen."

Worm spoke from the shadows of their flashlight beams. "Then why are we here?"

"Shut the fuck up, right now, Worm. We're doing no such thing. We're here to figure this thing out and get my fucking wife out of there. If that turns out to be a fool's errand, then we... I don't know."

Worm rumbled in the dark. "The one that came last, the seeker, the broken one, he won't be the last."

Nic saw Jacob's face, just inches from his own in the shadow and the gloom. His eyes squeezed shut and his head shook. "I don't have another plan. I've been in this black place for most of my life now. I can't remember the time before. I have to look at her picture to remember her face. I don't know what else to do..."

To the degree that Nic's mind could, it saw Laramie. Nic had only carried the weight of this alien abnormality for two days. The man in front of him had carried it for as long as Nic had been alive.

Janelle's voice cried out again, "I can't see! Is there anybody there?"

It echoed around them, in the time-space with them, around the outside of the walls around them, above and below, floating in time.

Laramie pulled Nick up to his feet, tears streaking his face.

"I can't tell you how many times I've heard that. Sometimes they say new things, but most of the time you just hear echoes of...things they said decades ago."

Nic whispered, "Can they hear us? Do they know we're here?"

Laramie shook his head, turned away, and motioned for Worm to keep going. After a few more turns, Worm glanced back at them, at Nic. "We're here."

Grady mumbled, whispered, and nodded, head bobbing back and forth like a mad owl. "You alone among the stars, you alone in the deep and dark."

He laughed, giggling like a small child who had won a game no one else could see. The black dread of the ghostly chorus was like hosannas to him. He shouted, "Yes! Yes! I come to perfect this world! To fulfill all of life! You alone among the stars! You alone in the deep and dark!"

He wasn't afraid; this might as well be his wedding day, his triumph, his crowning.

They snaked their way through the maze, Grady first, Worm second, and Jacob brought up the rear. Grady and Worm were cuffed, Laramie held a powerful flashlight in one hand and his revolver in the other.

As they reached the final door to enter the ballroom and leave the maze of ghosts behind them, Worm stopped short. "Please don't do this. Don't do this to him. I swear to the Mother and Father, to the deep places; don't do this to him."

Grady turned the doorknob to the ballroom and light filled the little place where they stood. He rushed in, gasping and chanting, "You alone among the stars! You alone in the deep and dark!"

Worm's back was to Laramie, and he pressed the barrel of his revolver into the big man's back. "I'll shoot you, Worm, and put him in that chair anyway. I don't want to hurt you any more, but I've got to know, I've got to find out. If that wall is a door to the...Room Between the Rooms, maybe...maybe it works both ways."

Worm shook his head, but didn't say anything.

Jacob pushed the barrel into Worm's back. "Then if you don't have anything else to say, start walking."

Worm walked several paces into the room, while Grady capered about, chanting, shouting, words devolving into mindless excited gibberish.

Jacob rasped, "Worm, stop. Don't take another step."

Worm stopped in his tracks. He didn't turn around.

Jacob leaned down and placed another set of open cuffs on the floor.

"Now slowly walk back, sit on the floor, and put those cuffs around your ankles. Do it now, or I will shoot you. This is your only warning. Say yes or no. Speak."

Worm stood for a moment, his shoulders shaking with sobbing. "Yessir."

He did as he was told. Jacob looked very carefully. The cuffs were secure.

Grady howled and whooped in the background, and Laramie caught Worm's gaze and held it. "I'm sorry, Worm, for the life you've had, for what's been done to you. I'm sorry for what I've done to you, but I've got to try. I've got to know."

Worm looked down and tears fell from his dirty face to the floor.

He didn't say anything.

Jacob turned his attention back to Grady, to the giant white marble room, to the steps leading down to the glass floor, to the raised dais with the heavy wooden chair and the raised pedestal before it, topped with a brass fitting, an odd slit in the middle.

Grady was already seated in the chair, his expression several shades of madness, the rictus grin cracking his bruised and scabbed face.

Laramie glanced back to Worm, who was still sobbing before the steps leading down to the glass floor, still chained.

Grady breathed in and out excitedly, an animal in heat. He gasped, "What are you waiting for? Unlock these and give me the *Clavis!*"

"First things first, Grady. You're going to answer my questions, honestly, or I'm just going to shoot you and be done with you. Do you understand?"

Grady leapt to his feet. "You fucking shit! You fucking nig—"

He was stopped short by the sound of Laramie's revolver.

He opened his eyes and realized he was still alive.

"That's your last warning. I'm giving you what you want, Grady. Now you give me what I want or all of your *fulfillment and perfection* is over. Do you fucking understand me, you hateful fuck?"

Grady, wild-eyed, sat back down.

"Good boy, Grady. That was close. Are you going to answer my questions or not?"

Grady glared alien daggers, but nodded his assent.

"Okay, is what you're sitting on the Throne of Knowing?"

Grady nodded. "Yes."

Laramie glanced down, through the glass, at the enormity of gleaming brass gears beneath.

"What is this thing beneath us?"

A note of hesitancy crossed Grady's face. "I'm not sure what it is."

Laramie nodded. "Give me an educated guess."

A creeping impatience came back to Grady's expression. "It's what...works the whole thing... I guess."

"How?"

Little shakes of the head. "I don't know, Laramie."

"Okay, how far down does it go?"

A blankness came to Grady's face. "All the way?"

"All the way to what?"

"I don't know."

Jacob paused. "The book didn't say?"

"It doesn't work that way. It only tells you what it tells you, and not in words."

"How did it get there?"

Grady stooped down and put his powerful flashlight against the glass. The beam cut through, but only illuminated what would be just a few stories down if this shaft was some sort of basement.

Every instinct told Laramie that this thing went down miles farther than that.

He whispered to himself, "That's impossible. That must weigh millions of tons..."

He turned back to Grady. "Answer me. How did it get there?"

Grady shook his head. "I don't know. Now uncuff me and give me the book."

Worm's voice cut through and Laramie whirled around to shoot, but Worm still sat, chained. "Dent called it down, the *Clavis* showed him how. That's what he told me before he went in there." He nodded to the blank marble wall before the seated Grady.

Jacob looked back and forth between the two chained men, baffled.

"It was always there, underground?"

Grady started giggling madly.

Laramie pointed the gun back to him. "Shut the fuck up."

He stopped, but the lunatic mirth still stamped his face.

Worm shook his head. "*No, he called it down.*"

Laramie squinted, then looked back to Nic, squinting at him. He nodded his head to the ballroom in front of them. "I don't know where the light comes from. There's no light sockets, no bulbs." He walked in and Nic hesitated, then followed.

"And I've never seen it go out, except once."

Nic turned and looked at him for a moment, then walked into the room.

Laramie reached out, as if to begin to say something, but his arm fell back to his side. No words were going to prepare Nic for the thing beneath the glass.

Worm sighed and lumbered over to the stairs and sat down, then looked down and closed his eyes.

Nic approached the stairs, then looked back to Laramie. Jacob nodded quietly. *Go on.*

Nic walked the few remaining feet to the stairs and looked down at what lay at the bottom. A glass floor, and an impossibility beneath. The out-of-place aspect of the raised dais, the heavy wooden chair, and the odd pedestal with the slit on top were completely lost compared to *it*.

Nic looked back again to Laramie. Jacob nodded again. "The glass is a few inches thick, you can walk across it."

Nic gingerly stood on the glass, then lowered himself to his hands and knees to peer through. He whispered over and over, "This is impossible, this is impossible."

Jacob continued, loud, as he walked forward, pulling something from his back pocket. "One time I shot my service revolver at it. All it did was chip it, it's that thick.

With one motion, he plunged the needle into the back of Worm's neck.

Worm jumped up, cried out, reaching for Laramie, and his knees gave way.

Nic screamed, "What are you doing, Laramie?"

Worm crumpled to the floor and Laramie was on his back, pulling his arms behind and cuffing him.

He quickly jumped down and put them on the big man's ankles.

"Nic, give me the backpack, right fucking now."

Nic did as he was told, bafflement and days of fear and confusion stamped on his features.

He stumbled over to Laramie, struggling to get the backpack off, and Jacob grabbed it from him, quickly unzipping it and pulling out a roll of electrical tape and a balled-up sock.

"I'm sorry about that, Nic, but the tranquilizer was only going to hold him for a few seconds, man of his size. I didn't want to give him too much and kill him, but...I guess we'll see."

He stood up and rolled Worm over onto his side to face Nic and the glass floor, dais, and chair behind him.

He gently, carefully, pulled a mat of hair away from Worm's face so he could see clearly. Worm lifted his head and moaned.

Jacob let out a big exhale and looked Nic in the eye. "We're almost there, almost there." He breathed in and out. "Thirty years... Thirty years without her and I'm an old man, but maybe, just maybe, we've got the key."

He unstrapped a length of tape and squatted behind Worm.

"Okay, Nic, unroll that thing and show it to Worm."

Nic stared back, utterly confused. "What...what are we doing, Laramie?"

Jacob exhaled hard again, practically panting now. "Okay, I didn't tell you the whole plan 'cause I don't know what happens next. Just do as I say. Unroll it and show it to him."

Nic looked down at Worm, then back up to Laramie. The old man nodded.

He shook his head, confused, then reached into the backpack to the thing rolled up and taped in cloth. He pulled aside the tape and unrolled it, then held up the Key of Perfection.

Worm's reaction was instant. He screamed like he was on fire: "No!"

Jacob strapped his mouth with electrical tape.

He stood up quickly. "We don't have much time, kid, and God bless you."

He looked down at the man, thrashing and kicking on the floor.

"God bless you too, Worm." His voice broke. "And I'm so sorry for what this life did to you."

He quickly took the book, the *Clavis Perfectum*, from the backpack and threw aside the ornately carved box.

He grabbed Nic by the arm and dragged him down the steps and across the glass floor to the raised dais. He pointed to the pedestal. "Stand there, and don't move until I tell you."

Nic broke. "What the fuck was that? What the fuck are we doing, Laramie?"

Jacob looked back. "We're standing on a giant lock. No one who ever went to the Room Between the Rooms ever came back. They didn't come back because they didn't have the key."

Grady grinned like a mad man, practically hopping up and down in the heavy wooden chair, what he said that the *Clavis* had referred to as the Throne of Knowing.

He laughed. "What are you waiting for? Let's get this show on the road!"

Jacob looked back to Worm, who had stopped crying and just stared forward, rocking back and forth.

He looked back to Grady. "Do you know what we do now? What we're supposed to do?"

Grady grinned, and it was even worse. "You uncuff me."

Laramie scoffed. "Ain't happening, shitbag."

Grady didn't miss a beat. "Then you give me the *Clavis* and we find out what's behind door number three."

He cackled, and it was abhorrent.

He turned behind him and pointed to the raised pedestal with the odd slit in its top. "What's this for?"

Grady's mirth fell, but just a notch. "The *Clavis* didn't say."

Laramie looked over the side of the raised dais at the glass floor and the enormity beneath. "It looks like it's the top, the point of that thing. Like...the very top of a skyscraper, just this one's underground..."

Grady whistled. "I don't know, and I don't care. Perfection is waiting while you moan like a fucking dipshit."

He looked back to Worm again, but he wasn't going to be any help; he was completely checked out.

It was just him and Grady. "If you fuck around, Grady, I will kill you."

Grady just looked at him. "How many times are you going to say that?"

Laramie exhaled hard, walked over to the big wooden chair, the Throne of Knowing, and set the key to the cuffs on the armrest.

He stepped back, revolver at the ready.

Grady shook with perverse joy as he unlocked the cuffs, taking a deep breath before setting his arms on the armrests. He turn to Jacob, then winked insolently.

Just as this happened, brass restraints snapped out of the armrests around Grady's wrists, then around his upper arms, then his calves, then his thighs. His smile could not get wider or more excited.

Laramie just stood there with his mouth open.

Grady turned to him. "You're just gonna catch flies like that, boy. Now set the *Clavis* in my lap."

Laramie stood dumbfounded for a moment, then noted that Worm had started sobbing once again. It crossed his mind that this was wrong, all wrong, but that was just another thing in a series of things that were all wrong.

He took the *Clavis* from its case and set it in Grady's lap.

Grady's body tensed, tightening. Laramie averted his gaze from the words on the pages, but observed that the effect was the same as before. The pages did not visibly turn, but Grady progressed through the book, seemingly in some sort of fast-forward.

Words began to form on Grady's lips.

At first, it was the familiar refrain of, "You alone among the stars, you alone in the deep and dark." But this changed too, becoming a series of monosyllables and automatic glossolalia.

Grady's body tensed further, becoming an awful automaton.

The syllables came quicker and quicker, blurring into a spell that sucked an essential something from the air. The light slowly dimmed, becoming a kind of darkness Jacob had never seen, even in the maze surrounding this place.

Blackness, darkness. Ancient, primal, from the time before the sun, before the stars. The kind that pulsed with a knowing of its potentiality. Of its purity. Of its potency.

And yet, he saw. The room limned in a purple phosphorescence.

A buzzing, like a million bees heard from beneath the waves.

A smell like burning hair.

And he saw. Above them in the air, a brass assembly of gears and wheels and rods. Turning on one axis, and another and another, the buzzing a sound of millions of teeth turning against one another, clicking into place, turning, grinding, locking and unlocking.

He didn't hear Worm coming up behind him, throwing his cuffed arms around him, pulling him, lifting him bodily in the air across the glass floor to tumble over the steps, wrestling him away.

Away from the thing that came next.

The terror as Grady came back into himself.

His screaming as he was deconstructed by a purple-limned cloud of gears in three dimensions, then four, then beyond until he was no more.

The blank marble wall before the Throne of Knowing flashed once.

The cloud of gears was gone. Grady was gone.

The *Clavis Perfectum* lay upon the raised dais just as Laramie had found it that first time, next to Janelle's purse.

Nic's heart pounded. He felt like he could faint. He felt like he could puke. He wanted to run, but he was sure Laramie would shoot him dead and try out his cosmic experiment without him.

One way or another, this was going to happen.

From his unreal thrashings, it was obvious Worm didn't think this was a good idea. His eyes bulged beneath the accumulated grime of moss and dirt. Veins were now visible on his skin and blood poured from his wrists as he strained to break free of the handcuffs.

"Laramie, he's gonna die if he keeps that up."

Jacob looked at Worm, years flashing over his eyes. Tears flew from his eyes too. He nodded. He whispered, "He won't die. He's stronger than you know. But he will break out of those cuffs and I will have to shoot him. I'm going to go in that room, and I'm going to get my wife. Either I walk out of here with her, or I don't walk out of here at all. I'm done with living, Nic. Not without her. Not anymore."

"I don't know if I can do this, Laramie."

"Son, you don't even know what you have to do yet. Now open that bag and get that stopwatch out and set it on the ground over there at the top of the steps. Somewhere Worm won't step on it when he breaks free. And start it. Go."

Nic quietly did as he was told, looking at Worm working his wrists back and forth with an equal measure of fear and pity.

Whatever was happening, whatever Laramie's plan was, he hadn't let Worm in on it because he suspected Worm would react this way, whatever *this way* was.

And Laramie had been right. Worm had recognized the Key of Perfection, knew what it was, whatever it was.

"What's the timer for, Laramie?"

Laramie was pasty with fear and anticipation; his breath came in short bursts, like a commander on a battlefield in the crucial moments when everything hangs in the balance.

"When I said that you mostly hear the ghosts saying the same things over and over... It's because, I think...I think time works different in the Room Between the Rooms. That's the reason I think Janelle may still be alive."

A stunned horror.

Nic stood there like a fool with his mouth hanging open.

Laramie grinned. "You trying to catch flies? You knew this was coming."

He grinned again and sat down on the Throne of Knowing with the *Clavis Perfectum* in his lap. As he did, brass restraints snapped in place at the wrists, upper arms, calves, and thighs.

The book flipped open to the first page.

"Don't look at it, turn away."

Nic whispered, averting his gaze, "Laramie, please—"

"And, Nic, take from this what you will, but you are a good person, you just had to find it. Now I'm going to look down and start reading. When I say, you take the Key of Perfection and you slide it in that pedestal there. I'm pretty sure it'll fit perfectly. Then you'll turn it."

"Laramie, seriously..."

Jacob looked down at the text in front of him. A spasm passed through his body, then another. The pages of the book didn't visibly turn, but somehow they flowed from beginning to end in a matter of seconds.

Laramie let out a prolonged and painful gasp.

Worm's thrashing increased, his head banging over and over against the floor as he tried to thrash his way over to them, and he rolled down the steps, leaving a red smear.

Laramie looked up at Nic in agony and ecstasy, blood vessels ruptured in his eyes. He panted, in and out. "Nic, put the key in there and turn it. Then drag Worm up those stairs." He panted. "If I'm not back in an hour, take that key and bury it where no one will ever find it."

Nic just stared. Laramie yelled, "Janelle! Please let me go to my wife, let me try, please, for the love of God, let me try."

Worm chewed through the electrical tape. "Stop! Stop!"

Nic looked once more at Laramie. The old man's watery blue eyes begged. His lips moved. "Please."

Nic turned around and slid the Key of Perfection into the slot atop the pedestal.

There was a sound that had never been heard before, at least not since the earliest man, if then. The sound of a machine, miles, maybe tens, maybe hundreds of miles in length. The sound of that machine turning. The sound of that machine awakening.

Nic turned to try to pull Worm away, but something had changed. All light had fled. He stood in a darkness deeper than he could comprehend. Laramie's flashlight still shone, but the darkness flowed around it, pushing the feeble beam of light back to its source.

Worm screamed, but the sound was muffled, then silenced.

Only the giant vibration of the machine continued, a resonance to shatter stone, to boil steel.

They were unmade, they were undone.

Nic opened his new eyes in a new place. He was on the ground, a stone place, dusty. The sky above was nothing but black clouds, blacker than he'd ever seen. Inky black, rippling and rolling.

Boiling...

He wasn't alone. Worm lay next to him, hyperventilating, eyes squeezed shut, head jerking back and forth. "No, no, no, no..."

He turned his head and looked around. This place was perfectly flat, extending to the horizon with no visible features. The ground was gritty, dusty, only a slight texture to the stone, but mostly gritty, mostly dusty.

Terribly dry.

The pedestal was before them, its white marble in stark contrast to the stone plain.

The chair sat behind him, heavy and wooden, restraints to the wrists, upper arms, calves, and thighs open. But Laramie wasn't in the chair.

Nic sat upright, squinting into the impossible distances above and around them. This was like no place on earth that he'd ever read about.

The ground was littered, here and there, with desiccated corpses.

Laramie was about twenty paces away.

He sat on the ground expressionless, cradling one of the dried-out bodies in his lap, rocking back and forth.

It was a woman, he could tell from the pink and yellow of her sundress, and the long black hair, dusty and ancient with time. She could have been here a thousand years if not for the wristwatch and simple gold ring around her finger.

Nic got to his knees, but could not bear to rise to his feet.

Laramie looked down to the withered face of his love, leaned down, and kissed her forehead.

He looked up after a moment, eyes clear.

His eyes met Nic's. "Thank you, son. Take Worm and go. Now turn away, this isn't for you."

He placed the revolver to his temple and fell down over the corpse of his love. His time was done.

Nic mouthed the word, but no sound came: No.

But the single shot did make a sound. It expanded out and over this eternal stone plain. Maybe it travelled around this eternal stone world, maybe not, but it echoed and kept echoing.

The clouds began to stir in their heavens. The boiling became a tempest, torn by winds, filling the air with inhuman screeching, high and low, of a million voices that wanted to be human, or had been human, but weren't.

A deep rumbling came from the ground, and he put his ear to the stone, to a sound like the very rock of this place was chanting an incantation in the language of this eternal stone plain.

He struggled to his feet and the earth shook.

He looked down on the ground at Worm rolling back and forth, mouthing, "No, no, no..."

The screeching from the sky grew in volume, and the clouds began to...separate, forming up into titanic ropy lengths that he swore bore a resemblance to tentacles.

They began to descend, and he was now convinced.

They were tentacles.

They searched the sky, writhing a hideous impossibility.

Every twitch of every muscle, and every twitch in time, their questing becoming more acute, more attuned.

He took a deep breath and reached down to the length of chain between the cuffs encircling Worm's hands.

The screeching from the skies turned toward him, and the tentacles unraveled, uncoiled, and descended, mile after mile.

He pulled with every fiber of his being and dragged Worm the last few feet to the pedestal. The tentacles came for them. The tentacles were upon them. He grabbed the key and turned it.

The screeching ceased.

He was slumped against the base of the chair. The room hummed and buzzed. He turned his head and looked down into the impossible abyss, and the machine that descended into its depths. It slowed its stirrings, the gears and rods snapped and slid into their final resting places.

It was still but for Worm, eyes clenched shut, still mouthing the words. "No, no, no."

The chair was empty, the restraints slid back into their hidden recesses.

Nic wobbled back to his feet. He saw that Laramie had left the key to the handcuffs on the armrest of the heavy wooden chair, the Throne of Knowing.

He took the key and gently unlocked the cuffs from Worm's wrists. His exertions had dug them all the way to the bone and the big man had lost quite a bit of blood.

He put the *Clavis Perfectum* back in its wooden box, and then its namesake, the Key to Perfection, rolled in its cloth, back into the backpack.

He put the stopwatch in his pocket, but didn't look at it.

He pulled Worm to his feet. "Worm, open your eyes. We've got to go bury these."

They walked back through the maze, but the ghosts said nothing, and neither did Worm. They arrived at the front door and grey daylight stung their eyes.

Grey, raining.

Flooded in places. Flooded like Nic had never seen in this part of Texas. This couldn't have happened in the amount of time they'd been inside Nelson Garvey's mad mansion.

He looked to Worm, confused. He pulled the stopwatch out of his pocket. It said they'd been gone for twenty-two days.

ABOUT THE AUTHORS

Curtis M. Lawson is a writer, poet, comic creator, editor, and musician. His published works include *Devil's Night, Black Heart Boys' Choir, The Coffin Maker's Book of Dark Tales,* and *The Envious Nothing.* He has also contributed to the writing and development of the TTRPG *Astro Inferno* from Haxan Studios. A key fixture at Weird House Press, Curtis serves as an editor and marketing director, and oversees the Gallows Whisper imprint.

Curtis resides on the outskirts of Providence, RI. In his free time, he pursues his passions of fitness and martial arts and records heavy music under the moniker IX of Blades.

Brett J. Talley is the author of several bestselling novels and anthologies, including *That Which Should Not Be*, *He Who Walks in Shadows*, and *The Fiddle is the Devil's Instrument*. He has been twice nominated for the Bram Stoker Award, the highest honor in horror fiction. He lives in Alabama with his wife, Annie, and their dog, Nyarlathotep, the barking chaos (Nyla for short).

Formerly a film critic, journalist, screenwriter and teacher, **Gemma Files** has been an award-winning horror author since 1999. She has published eight collections of short work, three collections of speculative poetry, a Weird Western trilogy, a story-cycle and a stand-alone novel (*Experimental Film*, which won the 2015 Shirley Jackson Award for Best Novel and the 2016 Sunburst Award for Best Adult Novel). Her collection *In This Endlessness, Our End* (from Grimscribe) won both the Bram Stoker Award and the This Is Horror Award in that category for 2021. Her collection *Blood from the Air* (also from Grimscribe) won the Bram Stoker Award for 2023.

William Holloway writes cosmic horror. He was born in Houston and lives in Austin. He is the author of the novels *The Immortal Body, Song of the Death God, Lucky's Girl,* and *Blackwood Estates,* and also of the novella *Ammonia* from the collection *The Abyssal Plain: The R'lyeh Cycle.* He is published by JournalStone and Weird House Press.

www.ingramcontent.com/pod-product-compliance
Lightning Source LLC
Chambersburg PA
CBHW030255270626
47156CB00022B/2762